I0553170

TEXAS COWBOY LAWMAN

BARB HAN

TorJake Publishing

To my family for unwavering love and support. I can't imagine doing life with anyone else.

CHAPTER ONE

Every U.S. Marshal had a doomsday plan. The one they half-joked, half-believed might be necessary someday, should the tables turn and one of them end up hunted by the dangerous felons they'd arrested. Most agreed their vehicles would be the first to go, along with cell phones. Smart tech and laptops; anything with a tracking device.

Those were obvious items and made everyone's list. Barrett Quinn added a few others to his, like ditching his credit cards and emptying his bank accounts into the offshore account he'd set up, just in case. Then there was the buried lockbox, with enough cash to get by for a few weeks, a fake ID, and a burner phone. Add an old pickup truck with fake tags, and he was all set. The plan was supposed to be theoretical, but he'd come close to needing one a few years back, so he refused to take any chances and kept it all up to date.

Enacting the plan meant a whole mess of lonely days and nights in his future, so he didn't take it lightly. The thought of no contact with his brother and best friend Harding was the pits.

Barrett sighed sharply as he tightened his grip on the steering wheel of the old Chevy. A whole lot had gone wrong for him to end up here, driving down this farm road at night, heading toward the interstate and to the one place no one would ever look for him.

Dirty Joe was to blame.

Dirty Joe Horowitz was infamous for shoving as much dirt as he could inside his victim's mouths, and up their noses, before killing them. The man was ruthless. Rumor had it that he'd once killed a close associate for accidentally spilling wine on Joe's favorite shirt in a restaurant. The associate had had too much to drink and became sloppy with his apology. The next morning, the man was found in the dumpster, bound and gagged with a mouthful of dirt. As was often the case, there was no way to tie the murder back to Dirty Joe. No fingerprints. No weapon. No DNA evidence.

The man was an efficient killer, who was known to hold a grudge, and he absolutely hated Barrett. He remembered the arrest well. Dirty Joe had been evading the law for two solid years after a warrant for his arrest had been issued. He'd been running his U.S. operation from the edge of the jungle near Bogota, Columbia, when Barrett came upon the encampment. Several days of observation, intense heat, and dehydrating sweat later, Barrett nabbed his target while the guy made his solo morning trek to empty his bladder. Dirty Joe's only downfall was his routine.

The personal threat against Barrett and his future children—should he ever have them—had been delivered through Dirty Joe's clenched teeth as Barrett handed the felon over to U.S. authorities. There was no doubt in Barrett's mind the man was capable of delivering on the promise personally, except that he was locked behind bars. Until two days ago, when he was spotted in Texas, no doubt on his way to Barrett's house.

There'd been threats before. They came with the job, as far as Barrett was concerned, and he couldn't fathom doing anything different other than working as a Marshal, so the whispered warnings never caused him to lose sleep at night. In fact, he was used to them, considering his job was to arrest the darkest of criminals. Those men and women who had nothing to lose because they were the 'lock 'em up and throw away the key' type of offenders.

He could count on one hand the number of times he paused when someone told him to watch his back. Dirty Joe was one of them. As a matter of fact, he was the only one. Within hours of his escape from Walls Unit—a.k.a. Huntsville Unit—the warden had contacted Barrett, saying that Joe's cellmate came forward with information about where Joe was headed. Since the cellmate didn't ask for anything in exchange, the information was deemed as righteous.

For the foreseeable future, Barrett needed to fly under the radar. The thought of going after Dirty Joe, rather than sit around and wait for him, had crossed Barrett's mind, but leaving town while his colleagues took over was a no-brainer. There was not a doubt in Barrett's mind that being home would only bring trouble to his neck of the woods. Going home to the family cattle ranch was also out of the question too. It would only bring heat and danger. Being out of reach and unable to contact would also prevent Joe from using any of Barrett's family members as hostages.

His brain short-circuited any time he thought about Joe being around his family. Barrett had notified them that he would be unreachable and, as much as he hated the thought of no communication, he had to stick to his word or put everyone at greater risk.

Everyone knew to be on guard. Harding had been the right messenger for the job. He ensured everyone stayed off the grid as much as possible. Folks knew to protect themselves. Plus, him hightailing it out of town kept Joe from wanting to stick around.

Still, Barrett couldn't help but worry about the worst-case scenarios. His thoughts were as heavy as thick gray rolling clouds during the threat of a spring thunderstorm in Texas. Add to the fact his nature went against tucking his tail between his legs and running the other way when trouble called, and it had all put him in one helluva sour mood.

Suck it up, buttercup.

Getting inside his head and churning over every possible scenario that could go wrong wouldn't solve anything. He'd learned that lesson the hard way years ago. Being tired all day as a result of lying awake in bed unable to sleep nearly got him shot once, so he learned real quick to put the previous day behind him before hitting the sack. Of course, it never hurt to have a beautiful woman by his side. However, he could admit the closer he got to forty, the number of people he wanted to spend time with on his days off shrank considerably.

He'd never seriously considered having a family, not with his lifestyle. The job was only part of the equation. He'd dated around enough to know his chosen career path shrank the dating pool applicants. This life wasn't for everyone. His brother Harding's new fiancé was a prime example of a great person who was not interested in being in a relationship with anyone who wore a badge. Lucky for Harding, love won the day.

The milestone birthday was probably messing with him, though. He could admit to feeling like something was missing in his life. Something he couldn't quite put his finger on. That 'something' would have to wait, now that he was on the run. Anger ripped through him at having to use his emergency plan and hoof it out of town like a hardened criminal. This nonsense wasn't supposed to happen to the good guys.

Another gut punch was staring into the abyss of loneliness. Being alone had never felt lonely to him until recently.

Barrett shook off the sentiment. No need to get mushy now. Harding had found true love and Barrett was genuinely happy for his brother. Being around his brother in his recent bliss shouldn't rub Barrett the wrong way; if anyone deserved happiness, it was Harding. Besides, Barrett had a full moon to keep him company tonight.

Driving on this stretch of road, there hadn't been one other vehicle in a solid hour. So, seeing a small sport utility parked off to the side of the road caught him off guard. Call him tainted—and he was—but there'd never been a time when coming up on a similar scenario was a good thing. Normally, it meant someone was about to get into trouble or arrested. Barrett reached for his Glock, that was secured underneath the driver's seat in its holster.

He flicked on his high beams and scratched his head. What was an abandoned vehicle doing out here this time of night?

The clock read half past two in the morning. Without much of a shoulder on this road, half of the SUV was in the scrub brush. Barrett sighed sharply. This was turning into one of those nights and his mood sure wasn't improving at this rate. Call it instincts honed after working in law enforcement, or just pure training, but he couldn't drive by the vehicle no matter how loud the little voice in the back of his mind yelled, *keep going*. The SUV was reasonably new and he highly doubted someone would have ditched it out here for no reason.

Barrett pulled onto the side of the road and trained his headlights onto the vehicle. He grabbed the flashlight he always kept in the dash—another one of those contingency plan items on his list—and stepped out of his vehicle. He checked the nearby field. Trees stood twenty yard off the road. It was possible someone parked here and stumbled out there, drunk. Could be a couple in search of privacy, or teens, or both. Why leave the vehicle here, though?

In this area of the country, wild boars regularly caused problems, not to mention black bears and coyotes. There were all manner of deadly insects, not the least of which was scorpions. The thought of snakes gave him the willies. He shut it down before his mind could go off the rails. Barrett hated snakes with a passion.

There was no sign of a human on either side of the road. He steadied himself, preparing for just about anything as he moved toward the vehicle. The SUV had Texas plates. If he had his department issue vehicle with laptop he could run those in a heartbeat. Considering the ones on his Chevy were fake, he also knew how easy it was to imitate the real deal.

The wind whipped around and the chill in the air said it was only going to get colder. November weather had always been a toss up. He took a few steps toward the vehicle with Glock and flashlight leading the way. The trunk space was empty. Same for the driver's seat. A hand came up to shield a female's eyes in the backseat. She had the seat back as far as it could go and was curled up on her side. Sleeping?

Barrett knocked on the window. Sleeping Beauty sat bolt upright as his finger hovered over the trigger mechanism. There was a decent amount of blood on her forehead that had run down the side of her face.

"Hands where I can see 'em," he said. No one should be out here this late at night, especially while bleeding.

With robotic movement, she complied. She didn't turn to look at him. Didn't need to for him to know her identity. This woman was trouble.

Even so, she looked to be in bad shape and needed help. Barrett tried the door, but it was locked. She reached for the button. A second later, he heard the tale tell click. As soon as he touched the door handle, she slumped over onto her side.

Barrett bit back a curse. There was no way he could

walk away from someone injured and in need of help. Leaving her alone out here might just end her life. She was vulnerable. But the senator's daughter was also news, and he couldn't afford to be seen with her.

————

Connie Owens blinked open blurry eyes. Pitch blackness surrounded her. She felt around to get her bearings as a headache the size of the Palo Duro Canyon took hold. Instead of her vehicle, she felt a comforter and sheets. There was a pillow underneath her head too. Strange.

The last thing she remembered—and memories were patchy at this point—she'd been driving down the road to get away from...

That's where her mind blanked and her brain cramped.

Fear caused her chest to squeeze as she recalled the shadow of a man appearing in the window of her vehicle. Was he the reason she was no longer in the SUV? Panicked, Connie felt around her body. Relief washed over her as she realized she still had her clothes on. Her hand went up to her forehead. Pain shot through her as she gingerly fingered the gash.

She stayed as still as humanly possible and listened as she tried to piece together what had happened prior to her ending up here. Wherever *here* was.

The bed was too comfortable to be a motel. The sheets weren't stiff. The hum of a heater said she was probably in a hotel room. But how?

Exhaustion tugged at the corners of her mind. She

tried to fight the urge to close her eyes, but the attempt was useless. A few seconds later, she was back under.

When she finally woke up properly, Connie had no idea how long she'd been in bed or how many times she'd opened her eyes, but enough sun peaked through the opening in the blackout curtains to tell her she'd successfully made it through the night. Sitting up proved far more difficult than she imagined. Slowly, one inch at a time, she managed an upright position. The male figure came to mind. All she remembered about him clearly was his size. He'd been huge.

Glancing around, she couldn't help but wonder if he had her right where he wanted her. A burst of anger fueled her enough to push off the covers. She threw her legs over the side of the bed and braced against the wave of nausea threatening to fold her in half.

The room started to spin as a door opened and a broad male figure filled the doorframe. The guy was big and muscled even though all she could see was his silhouette. It was enough to realize he wasn't the person who'd put the gash on her head.

"Did he send you?" she managed to ask. The question was stupid because she already knew the answer. And yet, she wanted to hear it from this jerk's lips. If she was going to die, she had a right to ask questions.

The figure walked across the room and she mentally recited the only prayer she could remember from her childhood. *Now I lay me down to—*

The light flipped on in the bathroom and the door cracked.

"I'd open the curtain, but it's bright outside. Based on the gash on your head, I'd say you suffered a mild concussion at the very least. Light won't be your friend for the next couple of days," the strong male voice sent vibrations rocketing through her. Then came, "Who is this *he* you're referring to?"

"Do you know who I am?" she asked without answering his question.

"Ms. Owens," he responded.

"How do you know me?" she asked, hoping he could help her piece together what had happened, and why she was alone in a hotel room with a stranger. He leaned against the wall next to the bathroom door. From here, all she could see were shadows across his face. From what she could see so far, the man was gorgeous. Didn't mean he wasn't dangerous or wouldn't kill her, though.

"I'm pretty sure everyone who lives in Texas knows who the senator's daughter is," he said, folding his arms across a chest that would make Marvel superheroes jealous.

Hearing the words *senator's daughter* sent a cold chill racing down her back. She nodded, more curious than ever who this man was and why they were in the same room together.

"You're going to have a fill in the gaps for me," she said, figuring she had no reason not to trust this man. "My memory is spotty. Do I know you?"

"I doubt it," he said with a chuckle that was a low rumble in his chest. Based on his size, she should feel very afraid to be alone in a room with him, and yet there was something about him that put her at ease. Though probably every serial killer victim felt the same way right before the ax dropped. "My name is Barrett."

Interesting that he didn't offer his last name. The

same voice that told her to trust him also urged her not to push for information. He must have a reason as to why he didn't want to share his last name. The thought reassured her. If he intended to kill her, there would be no reason not to tell her everything about him. But also, wouldn't she already be dead?

"Are you helping me?" she asked, trying to make out the details of his face. From what she could tell so far, the man was drop-dead gorgeous. Then again, her brain was still foggy and her vision blurred. He could be a figment of her imagination for all she knew.

"As much as I can," he stated. "I found you on the side of the road in your SUV. You have a serious gash on your forehead and you seemed like you needed a friend."

"Is that what you are?" she asked. "A mystery man who saves stranded women on deserted roads?"

Barrett didn't speak for a long moment. He just stood there almost as though contemplating what he should reveal. This man had secrets and a growing part of her wanted to know what they were.

"I managed to get a few supplies. There's a couple of muffins in the other room and I can put on a fresh pot of coffee. It's not much, and it's not great, but I can get another couple of cups out of it. Then I'd like to take a better look at your injury before I head out," he said, with finality in his voice.

A sense of panic overwhelmed her at the thought of doing all this alone again. But she couldn't exactly tell her story to this stranger. In fact, she hadn't decided for herself how to best handle the situation she'd found herself in the other night.

"A muffin would be nice," she conceded. "Coffee would be heaven. Even if it's awful."

"I have banana and blueberry. Wasn't sure what you liked," he said. Getting both because he didn't know her preferences weren't the actions of someone who wanted to harm her. In fact, it was very thoughtful.

"Thank you," she conceded. "For that and the comfortable bed. I slept all night."

His eyebrow shot up.

"All night?" he parroted. "You've been out for a day and a half."

Shock didn't begin to describe the emotions running through Connie. She'd lost track of the days and nights. And if the information in her possession ever came to light, she risked a whole lot more.

CHAPTER TWO

"Do you need help up?" Barrett asked, figuring Connie might need a steady hand.

She shook her head but there wasn't a whole lot of confidence in her expression.

"I'll get out of here and let you clean up. There's a toothbrush on the sink still in the wrapper. I brought in your suitcase but didn't go through any of your things, so I wasn't sure what you needed," he said.

"My purse?" she asked as her delicate eyebrow arched.

"It's on the chair over there," he pointed to the corner but it was too dark over there to see clearly.

"This is amazing," she said with a whole lot of gratitude in her voice. There was tension too. He'd been expecting it, considering the blow to her head and the fact he was a stranger. Then came, "I'm not sure how I can repay your kindness."

"No need," he said. "I had hoped to get you back on your feet before I head out."

"Mind if I ask where you're going?"

The question caught him off guard. "It's best if I don't give a whole lot of details about me," he said after a pause. "In fact, you'd be better off forgetting that I exist once we go our separate ways."

"Oh," she said, sounding deflated. It was almost like a balloon quickly losing air. "I'll respect your privacy and be happy that you stopped to render aid."

"That's all I can ask and is best for both of us," he confirmed. She didn't need to be tied up with a man being hunted by Dirty Joe.

"Banana," she said before adding, "my favorite muffin."

Barrett smiled and nodded. He'd paid the downstairs clerk under the table in cash for the room. He couldn't risk using anything from inside her wallet without knowing how much trouble she was in and why. And, frankly, hadn't wanted to get his fingerprints on any of her personal belongings, considering her family's political background and the fact her father had all but announced he was making a bid for the presidency. Using his own identity was out of the question. He had a fake ID but no credit cards to match.

The first thing Barrett had done once he got her to bed was to go into the living room of the suite to check the news. If Connie was drugged out and missing, it would have made news. Of course, a politician running for president would most likely have the means to suppress any information that might damage the campaign.

Barrett could admit to being curious as to why the

senator's adult daughter seemed on the run. Despite the heavy makeup and tight clothes, he'd recognized her instantly. How could he not? Their family portraits were all over the media and it made sense once rumors began that Senator Owens had grand plans for his future—a future that involved an even more public life than the one they already had. Barrett couldn't imagine living in a bigger fishbowl than the one where he'd grown up. Quinns were known entities in and around Texas, but politicians were on a whole new level. The other thing their families had in common was expectations. He knew all about those too.

Connie Owens seemed to live a clean life, so he was scratching his head as to why she would need to hide out. Then again, he was a lawman and former cattle rancher. The world of politics played on a whole different field—one he had no intention of suiting up for. Plus, the senator's daughter was news. Any random person with a cell phone and a social media account who spotted her could reveal Barrett's location.

Since he couldn't rightly leave her until he knew she was okay and could fend for herself, he'd committed to sticking around. When she came out of the bedroom, he wanted to address her injury. The fact she'd slept so much had had him on the edge of his seat. Several times over the course of the past thirty-six hours he'd almost wiped the place clean of his own fingerprints, called 911, and got out of there. His conscience had stopped him.

Connie emerged from the bedroom in a night-sky blue velvet jogging suit that hugged her curves. She was short by Quinn standards, he guessed around five feet

six inches. Her wavy auburn hair was pulled off her face
and had been wrangled into a ponytail. Much of the
dried blood had been washed from her face, leaving
nothing but creamy skin. Honey-brown eyes stared at
him as she walked over to the kitchenette and sat down
in the chair he motioned toward. His heart took a hit at
seeing her. She was beautiful. He'd noticed it right away
in the vehicle despite the makeup. But now? He could
clearly see the long, thick eyelashes framed eyes he
could stare into for days. It didn't stop there. She had
full cherry tinted lips that he needed to stop staring at,
no matter how much they begged to be kissed.

He poured two cups of coffee after fixing her up
with a banana muffin. After setting a cup in front of her,
he took the seat across the table and picked up his cell
phone. "Once you feel human again, I'd like to take a
look at your forehead."

"Okay," she said in between bites. She was making
quick work of the muffin, so he grabbed an apple that
he'd planned to eat and set it down in front of her
instead. "Is that for you?"

"Not really. I bought supplies for both of us," he
said.

"Why are you still here?" she asked, curling one leg
underneath her sweet bottom while she studied him.

"What do you mean?" he figured playing dumb
would buy him a little time to come up with honest
answers that made her less curious about what he was
doing and why he was on the farm road in the middle of
the night in the first place.

"First of all, you didn't have to stop and check on

me," she said. "Though, I'm forever grateful that you did."

"You're welcome," he said before taking a sip of his coffee. Her lips compressed and she took in a quick breath. He knew before she opened her mouth to speak something was bugging her.

"I'm serious when I say you went above and beyond," she stated. "And so I don't want to come across as ungrateful."

"Okay," he said.

"What made you stay?" she asked as one of her delicate eyebrows arched.

"You were injured, for one," he stated.

"Fair," she said. "Why not drop me off at an ER and bolt out of there?"

"I wanted to know that you were all right before I headed out," he admitted. It was true. "Plus, you seemed like you were running from someone. I didn't want him to catch you while you couldn't defend yourself."

"Much appreciated," she said as she studied the rim of her paper coffee cup. "It's not a boyfriend, in case you were wondering."

"None of my business," he said, quickly. Too quickly? The short answer was yes, even though he could admit to being curious as to whether or not she was in a relationship. He had no business being attracted to Connie. And he had no plans to stick around, so even if she was just as drawn to him, as he was to her, it wouldn't work. She was news and he needed to stay under the radar. Period.

"I just didn't want you to think I would get into a

relationship with an abuser," she said, as she slowly lifted her gaze to meet his. "I don't know why that's important. It just is."

The moment their eyes met, a fireworks show went off inside his chest. *Way to play it cool, Quinn.* This was about as close to pathetic as he'd ever been. His heart pounded against his ribs from the inside and he was fighting a Texas-sized attraction to a woman he'd stopped to help.

"Is your family worried about you?" he asked, knowing full well he shouldn't be putting on his investigator hat.

She issued a grunt.

"Yes, but not for the reasons you might think," she said incredulously. Her answer was loaded, and he knew better than to follow along the trail.

"I'm sorry," he said, "Families can be difficult to navigate."

"You have no idea," she said in a tone that warned him not to ask.

"Do I want to?" he continued, forcing logic aside. For reasons he couldn't begin to explain, Connie had gotten under his skin. He was concerned about her on a personal level. In his work, he'd become a little too good at compartmentalizing. It helped him do his job— a job he was good at. On the emotional side, it wasn't so great. Those tight boxes didn't want to stay shut off from the world forever, and he had no idea how to have a real conversation about all the information locked inside.

Where was this coming from?

Barrett had been off the job for two days and he was already getting philosophical? *Seriously, Quinn?*

From somewhere deep, he realized this had to do with being around Connie. What was it about two strangers being stuck in a hotel room together that made sharing secrets seem like a good idea? It wasn't, he reminded himself. In fact, it was the worst of the bad ones.

———

Connie leaned forward, resting her elbows on the edge of the table. Based on Barrett's expression, he looked like he might be close to sharing something real about his life. There was no logical explanation for why it seemed so important to her to know this man on a personal level, except he had most likely saved her life. It felt important to know something about him in return. Besides, her 'fairy tale' life had been broadcast on every news station, blog, and newspaper. Appearances weren't everything.

When he issued a sharp sigh, her shoulders deflated.

"My life isn't like anything you've been told or have seen on TV," she said, picking up her coffee and holding the warm cup in her palms. She had to be gentle or risk the paper cup folding or crinkling on her, spilling its contents. The warmth she felt right now was worth the risk.

"Do you want to explain why?" he asked before putting his hands up, palms out, in the surrender position. "It's none of my business, so I'm not trying to stick my nose where it doesn't belong."

"I offered the information," she said. "You're not exactly prying."

"Just so we're clear," he stated. "Which is to say that I respect your privacy."

"Well, I sure appreciate it," she said. "Growing up in the public eye caused most folks to feel like they both knew me and had a right to know my every move."

"I know exactly what you're—"

He stopped himself midsentence and for a split second, she wondered who his people were. Did she know them? He hadn't offered his last name, so he must not want her to know who he was. She'd been around enough bodyguards and law enforcement to notice he carried himself like one. They walked differently. Always with a gun at their hip, they naturally kept their arms extended away from their bodies more than most, even when they weren't carrying.

Connie couldn't help but study his face and the hard lines that contrasted thick, full lips.

"Having eyes on you all the time isn't easy," he finally said.

"No," she agreed. "It is not. And people think they know what's happening, but they have no idea what goes on behind closed doors."

She wished she could tell him exactly what that meant, but there was no way she planned to involve a stranger in her worst nightmare.

"Pardon my saying so, but you're old enough to live on your own, and you most likely have your own life. Doesn't the press die down at some point?" he asked.

"It did until recently," she stated. "I do have my own place and would very much like to have my own life."

"The presidency?" he asked, but his eyes said he already knew the answer.

"Suddenly, it's like I'm on trial," she said, biting her tongue before she said something she might regret. If only people knew. Then again, what she knew could kill her, and she had no idea what to do next. "Everything I say or do is captured and sold or printed. But, you know, I've grown up with it, so even though it's a whole lot more intense, it's not how I ended up in the vehicle last night." She realized she'd said too much the instant his eyebrow shot up. A wrinkle of concern scored his forehead. Rather than wait for him to react further, she said, "Do you mind taking a look at my injury while we're here?"

He hesitated for a moment before saying, "Sure thing."

"I don't have any—"

"No trouble," he interrupted. "I travel with a first-aid kit and what I didn't already have, I bought when I went out for supplies yesterday."

"I know I've said this more times than I can count already, but thank you," she said, realizing he put himself on the line to make this pitstop with her. She shot a furtive glance in his direction as he stood up and retrieved a bag, along with a bright orange case the size of a small suitcase. Barrett seemed prepared for almost any situation, which only brought up more questions. Someone who worked in law enforcement, who was now on the run caused all kinds of scenarios to pop up in her mind.

First things first, she instinctively knew she could trust him.

She'd been passed out for a day and a half, and he could have done anything he wanted during that time. What did he do? Made sure there was food when she woke up. Bought supplies to treat her injuries and stop her from getting an infection.

"I would have already worked on this. You were out cold and the last thing I wanted to do was to have you wake up to a stranger bent over your face, so I made the decision to leave you in peace," he explained on the way back from across the room.

Again, Barrett had been nothing but thoughtful.

"I'm not sure I made the right call," he continued. "Looks like your injury is trying to get infected."

The two-inch gash that ran along the right side of her hairline would most likely leave a scar.

"Mind telling me how this happened?" he asked as he set down the supplies on the table.

She turned her chair to face him and when he stepped close enough for their legs to graze, a jolt of electricity like nothing she'd ever experienced shot through her body, alighting senses she didn't even know existed.

"I-uh," she stammered as her mouth dried up. She cleared her throat and continued, "That's the wild thing...I can't remember. At first, I thought it might have been the press—they've chased my vehicle more times than I can count—but that doesn't feel right, and I have no memory of being struck. In fact, the last thing I remember is having coffee at this little place that I love in downtown Austin. I have no idea how I ended up wearing the outfit I had on. Most days, I put on enough makeup to stop the press saying that I look pale, but that's about it. And I don't know who specifically I was running from, which is the only explanation for where you found me."

Connie knew who was responsible for her needing to be on the run, though. She would never forgive or forget, but she needed to find a way to get the information she had to her mother, so she could escape too.

CHAPTER THREE

"Someone might have slipped something into your drink." Barrett clenched his back teeth at the thought anyone would do that to another human being to make them compliant, but his job had brought him face-to-face with the worst in people.

"I guess so," Connie said on a shrug as she tilted her face toward him.

Methodically, he cleaned the area around the gash while being as gentle as he could.

"Did you go to the bathroom after receiving your order? Leave your drink alone for any amount of time?" he asked, unable to stop the investigator in him.

"No," she said. "I was reading a book and I distinctly remember not being able to put it down. By the time I finished the couple of chapters at the end, my cup was drained."

"I'm guessing the cup was never outside of your view either," he said.

"It sat right in front of me the whole time," she

admitted. "No one could have walked by and slipped something in without me noticing. My table was in the corner, so someone would have had to go out of their way to walk over."

"That was going to be my next question," he admitted. "Do you want advice on how to go about investigating who did this to you?"

She winced as he blotted the wound.

"Sorry," he said, hating the fact he'd just hurt her when he was trying to help.

"It's fine," she said, reaching a hand up to close around his. She squeezed for a brief second, but the aftershocks from their physical contact would live in his body for a long time. It was the equivalent of a lightning strike on a sunny day, random and shocking all at the same time. His heart jumpstarted and, for the first time in a very long time, he could feel it beat in his chest. An attraction of this magnitude wasn't the problem. Heck, he'd welcome it as proof he was still alive. But the timing was more than unfortunate. It was downright depressing. Besides, he was running from a known enemy and she was running from something at the very least partially unknown. Running into each other's arms would be a mistake.

The magnetic attraction was probably nothing more than two souls bonding over similar circumstances. Not to mention, Connie was beautiful. After talking to her, he could tell she was intelligent; brains and good looks were a powerful combination in his book.

Barrett finished up by applying antibiotic ointment.

"Since your hair is already pulled off your face, I'd probably let the wound breathe. I can teach you how to dress it for bed, or drop you by a doc in the box or ER if that suits you. I'm no professional, but you probably needed stitches," he surmised, figuring she could take the advice or leave it. He put it out there just the same.

"This is good," she said. With hurt in her eyes, she locked gazes. "Does that mean you're leaving soon?"

"Sticking around in one place for too long wouldn't be good for my health," he said, trying not to give away too much. The less she knew, the better. Still, the mix of disappointment and sadness in her eyes hit him square in the chest.

"What are you hiding from?" she asked outright, her eyes pleading for an answer that he couldn't give.

"Suffice it to say, it's not safe to be around me," he stated.

"Did you do something wrong?" she pressed.

"Nope," he said. "But that doesn't mean I'm not dangerous."

"You're not to me," she said.

"Not directly, no," he conceded.

"I could say the same to you about me," she continued and he wondered where she was going with this. "All I'm saying is that we both might have a better chance if we combined forces."

"You have no idea what you're saying, or who you're saying it about," he stated. A voice in the back of his mind pointed out that Dirty Joe was after Barrett, not Connie. Wouldn't that keep her safe should Dirty Joe find them? Of course, the best-case scenario had the law catching Dirty Joe by nightfall. Barrett would have to learn about it over the news, because he hadn't left his brothers or cousins with a good phone number to reach him. He couldn't. It was too risky. They couldn't know anything about his whereabouts or have any way to reach him. This was the plan.

"You're right about that, Barrett," she said before adding, "if that's your real name."

"It is," he reassured. The other thought that dawned on him was a guy like Dirty Joe would use anything and everything against Barrett. If Joe believed Connie was important to Barrett...he didn't want to go there about the ways in which Dirty Joe would use the information against Barrett. Ruthless and cold-hearted weren't the terms he wanted associated with someone who came into contact with her.

"That's a good place to start," she said. "I can see that you're a good man. There's no way you would stop to help a stranger, and then do all this for her, unless you were decent and honest."

"It seemed like the right thing to do at the time," he said, thinking he wasn't so certain bringing her here had been his best move. Now that she was awake and talking, she had questions. He was beginning to realize that she didn't seem the type to give up without finding answers, digging her heels in until she got what she wanted. Normally, he admired that in a person. The trait was too rare as it was. In this case, it could put her in the line of fire and he couldn't have her death on his conscious. "Believe me when I say you'll be far worse off if I stick around much longer, though."

"Couldn't we figure this out together? Stay here until—"

"The clerk here can give anyone who walks through the front door a description of me and he's the only one who knows we're in this room. His bosses don't. His co-workers don't. I paid for this room in cash and under the table," he said. "I'd like it if you forgot what I looked like and that I stopped to help you. It's the best way to repay me."

"Whatever you want," she said, and he could feel a sudden chill in the air. He honestly wasn't trying to hurt her feelings. His intentions were the opposite. He was trying to keep her alive.

"I can drive you back to your vehicle or to the ER like I said before," he continued, ignoring the stabbing pain in his chest and the feeling he'd betrayed his best friend.

"Back to my vehicle is fine," she said. "I can't risk going to the hospital or being seen any more than you can."

"Because of the person who hit you on the head?" he asked even though he should leave the topic alone.

"Something like that," she murmured. "Does it matter?"

"It does to me," he said before he could reel the words back in. "I understand this seems one-sided. I'd probably react the same way if the situation was reversed. Believe me when I say not knowing who I really am is the best favor I can do for you."

"Then I'm at a loss, because you already know who I am," she said with a shrug.

"I have no idea why you're out here with me and I'm doing my level best not to ask too many questions, which goes against my nature," he said with a slight smile, trying to ease some of the tension between them.

"I've taken up enough of your time," she said after a

long, thoughtful pause. "You've been nothing but kind to me, so I don't want to repay you by being difficult. I probably wouldn't be alive right now if it wasn't for you, so I'm grateful. Take off whenever you need to. Believe me when I say that I understand not being able to share secrets. It's probably for the best if we leave it at that."

He was the one who needed it to be like this, so why did her sudden dismissal hurt like hell?

———

Connie grew up in a political family. She'd witnessed maneuvers and battles firsthand. So, she also realized when a fight had been lost. She truly was grateful to Barrett. It wasn't right for her to ask more of the man. Besides, an unwelcomed attraction was the last thing she needed on her plate.

"I'd like to stay until I know you can handle being on your own," Barrett said. His consideration was only making him more attractive.

"I'll figure it out," she said. "When is a good time to take me to my vehicle? And, by the way, where is it?"

"I drove it behind the tree-line to hide it from the road," he said as she did her level best not to look straight into those intense eyes. She feared it would be like looking directly at the sun and would damage her retinas in the same way he threatened to damage her heart if he stayed. This was probably for the best.

"Oh, good. Hopefully, no one has found it," she said. "Should we wait until nightfall to make a move?"

"Dusk should be a good time," he said. "I'd like to get there before the sun goes down, so we can do a visual sweep of your vehicle to make sure it's safe for you to get inside."

"Okay." Connie noted how much he sounded like law enforcement. "In the meantime, I had to get rid of my cell phone so I couldn't be tracked."

"Is the vehicle yours?" he asked.

"No," she said. "It belongs to a...friend."

"Can it be traced to the friend?" he asked.

"It's unlikely but not impossible," she said. "Let's just say families who are always in the spotlight develop individual plans of how to disappear."

"And you are no exception," he pointed out.

"Right. My only hiccup is a family member is involved in this, and I have no idea how much he knows about my personal life," she said, realizing she'd probably gone too far.

"Your father?" he asked with a raised eyebrow.

"*Step*father," she corrected.

"I didn't know he wasn't your biological parent," Barrett said. "I can count on one hand what I know about your family but that catches me by surprise."

"He adopted me and changed my last name," she said. "I didn't even know the man wasn't my real father until I was in college."

"That must have been a shock," he said with sympathy.

"After knowing my stepfather for most of my life, I wasn't as surprised as I should have been," she said. "The makeup, the dress, the attack. I have no idea how or why, but I know he is behind this."

"How can you be so certain?" he asked.

Since the two of them were about to part and never

see each other again, she figured it wouldn't hurt to unburden herself with at least part of the truth. As it was, the world knew Hunter Owens III as a family man and a model husband. Connie knew different, and what she had on him would blow his image sky high.

"I have proof," she said, and it was like the boulder that had been docked on her chest since she'd witnessed her stepfather giving a kill order and saying she meant nothing to him. She was a liability to his career.

"This is why you're on the run," he muttered mainly to himself because she could scarcely hear the words.

"Yes," she answered anyway. "Until I come up with a plan to get my mother out of there and away from him, I'm stuck."

"How do you know she'll leave?" he asked.

"I don't," she stated honestly. "But I can tell you that she has no idea what the man is doing and what he's capable of. I overheard her speaking in hushed tones to one of her friends, saying something about wishing she had freedom."

"You're thinking you can blackmail your stepfather?" he asked.

"I need to stay alive for a few days so I have time to figure it out," she admitted. "This is all new to me and he knows. I'm certain he's sending one of his henchman to do his bidding and erase me. How sympathetic would the public be to a man losing a daughter who they believe is all about family?"

"Politicians have used less to be catapulted into the highest office," he said on a sharp sigh.

"Exactly," she confirmed. "My death would have to look like an accident."

"Or a tragedy," he said. "Based on what you've told me so far, the makeup and tight dress might have been meant to make it look like you'd spiraled out of control."

"I could see him manipulating that into making folks believe his family is fallible, just like everyone else's," she said. "The thought makes me want to throw up."

"He doesn't seem to care about your reputation," he stated.

"No. I'm expendable to him," she said. "So is my mother. I'm one hundred percent certain he's had affairs. Meanwhile, my mom has been faithful." She had heard her mother whisper the name Thorogood Hammond, but it was unlikely her mother was having an affair. Right?

"As far as you know," he said.

She blinked a couple of times. "Actually, you're right. She has survived this long living with a snake."

"She would come up with ways to cope," he said. "Maybe even figure out how to carve out a life for herself while her husband does his thing."

"When you put it like that, I hope she has," she said. "Do you know how my stepfather got his first seat in the senate?"

Barrett shook his head.

"I had a brother," she said, the memory still raw after all these years. Tears threatened even after all this time.

"Wait," he said. "I remember something about this in the news. He passed away, didn't he?"

She nodded, surprised at the emotion clotting her

throat. She'd been trained from a young age to look the part but had never truly been allowed to grieve. "He dragged me and my mother out of the house for a press conference."

"You stood there with a teddy bear dangling from your hand," he said. "I remember that now like it was yesterday."

"The press had a field day with me in my black raincoat, holding Teddy's hand," she said, a queasy feeling took hold. "The bear belonged to my brother. No one knew that and my stepfather sure never corrected them. He just let them go on believing it was mine. The truth is that he handed it to me right before we walked outside for the press conference, and asked me to hold it."

"He exploited the pain of an eleven-year-old, and the press wasn't any better," he said with the same bitter look she felt in her bones. "I'm truly sorry you went through that. It was a terrible loss and no one should ever have to lose someone they love so young."

Those words, spoken with such compassion, were balm to a wounded soul. Connie had no idea why she was spilling her secrets to Barrett, except to say she felt safe around him and a growing part of her wanted him to know the real her. She'd been forced to wear a public face as far back as she could remember, and it felt like high time to set the record straight with at least one person.

"Mitchel was eight years old when the boating accident happened on Lake Travis," she continued as Barrett moved next to her and then took a knee. He reached out and took her hand in his. The electricity was instant and powerful. Instead of zapping her strength, the connection gave her a renewed energy to keep going. "He was my stepfather's biological child and I don't think I saw the man shed a tear except for the cameras."

Barrett didn't speak. No words were needed. His compassion was stamped all over his features and it radiated from him in palpable waves. He drew circles on the palm of her hand with his thumb. The motion spread warmth like a fire, circulating through her, consuming her, making her feel like everything might actually turn out all right.

"I can only imagine how horrible it must have been for you," he said after a pause. "Any man who exploits his children like that should be locked up and thrown behind bars."

"I couldn't agree more," she said. Now, she had the evidence to do just that, but first she had to figure out a way to pull her mother out of the man's clutches so she couldn't be collateral damage.

CHAPTER FOUR

Barrett was in trouble. If he was smart, he would stop this conversation before his heart overruled logic—logic that told him to take a step back. He needed to distance himself as much as possible because the more he got to know Connie, the more he wanted to help. Helping her was one of the fastest ways to expose his true identity. He might as well give Dirty Joe the hotel's address and have someone hold the elevator for him. Walking away from Connie was going to haunt him even though that was exactly what he had to do.

"What happened with my mom was worse," Connie continued. "She lost the spark in her eyes after losing my brother. The wine glass came out at dinner and kept full with steady refills until she passed out. It was as if she was just hollowed out."

"Losing a child has to be the most unnatural thing in the world, and the cruelest," he said. "Most folks don't recover."

She nodded as a tear rolled down her cheek. He

brought his free hand up to thumb it away, creating the most intimate moment he'd experienced in far too long.

Justice was something Barrett took seriously. Hearing about a crooked senator wasn't a huge surprise, but knowing the details and seeing the callousness of the man's actions riled up Barrett in more ways than he could count. Sure, it was his job, but his job was more than just a career. His life's work was to ensure justice was served, and bad people were kept off the streets and away from law-abiding folks. It sounded cliché, but he got into law enforcement to make a difference.

Barrett loved his home state. Texas, the land, the wide-open skies were all ideals that deserved honoring and respecting. So, he was riled up even further that a jerk like Hunter Owens III was the representation of those ideas, when the man didn't walk the talk.

And then there was Connie and her mother. Two people who didn't deserve the fate life had handed them, in losing their brother and child. For a father to exploit his son's death for political gain made Barrett angrier than he cared to admit. Thankfully, he'd gotten his temper under control years ago at the ranch and on the football field. Hard, physical labor and sports were a teenage boy's best friends.

Connie took in a sharp breath before standing up and crossing the room.

"Thank you for listening to me," she said. "I've never talked about him before with anyone."

"No need to thank me," he said, wishing he had some magic words to make everything better. He'd never felt so helpless in all his life. There wasn't much else he could do but listen.

"It'll be dark soon enough. I'll get my bag together and we can get out of here," she said as he felt a wall come up between them that he didn't know how to break through. She'd been through hell and back, and he respected her even more now that he knew the truth. To outsiders, families could look so different than what they really were behind closed doors. He couldn't say that he knew a whole lot about the Owens family, aside from their public spit-shined image. When he really thought about it, his own family probably looked similar to onlookers. Recently, they'd healed old wounds between his father and uncle, wounds that ran deep, but Barrett wasn't particularly close to his own father and neither was Harding.

In fact, he couldn't remember the last time he'd spoken on the phone to his father, or even in person. There were no calls to check in and see how his sons were doing from former Sheriff Quinn. Funny, Barrett didn't even think about his father much. Was that a job hazard or just a way of life?

Either way, he didn't figure the lack of relationship factored into his day-to-day much. He had Harding and his other brothers. He'd grown up close to his cousins. There was enough testosterone in Barrett's life to make up for his father's failings.

While Connie gathered her things in the next room, he figured it best if he did the same. He packed a couple of meals of protein bars and fruit for Connie, before doing the same for him. She would also need a small medical kit, which he put together next.

By the time she re-entered the living room, he had everything stacked on the table and ready to go. The look of hurt and disappointment in those honey-browns would haunt him for the rest of his life. If something happened to her now, he'd never forgive himself. If he could take her with him...he wouldn't hesitate. Separating was for her own good, even though she didn't seem to see the decision in the same light. She had no idea who he was up against. Her stepfather might be ruthless with subterfuge, but Dirty Joe would have no qualms about a public display of murder.

It seemed a shame not to share more about him with her. Connie was someone he actually could see himself opening up to, which was a shocker. First of all, Barrett wasn't the talkative type. And then there was the fact talking about his personal life was right up there with having his eyebrows waxed. Both sounded beyond painful, and like a terrible idea.

"Ready," she said, gripping the handle of her overnight bag like it might explode if she let go.

There was something about her standing there, chin up, looking ready to brave the loneliness they both knew was coming that gutted him. A coil tightened in his chest at the thought of going their separate ways. There would be no way to contact each other and the only way he had a chance at figuring out if she was okay or not would be the news. The coil tightened, making taking in a deep breath next to impossible.

Barrett had to remind himself to breathe slowly before wiping down the room to ensure there were no fingerprints left behind.

"Then let's go," he said, needing to get it over with, as opposed to dragging out a goodbye that was only going to make the coil even tighter. "Look, your stepfather has folks looking for someone single, so is it okay if I put my arm around you as we walk out? I should also hold your bag since all I have is a backpack. We'll draw less attention if folks believe we're a couple. The more intimate we seem, the more people will look in the opposite direction."

Connie nodded before handing over her bag. She picked up the plastic grocery bags filled with supplies. The fact she'd stopped speaking to him was probably a survival tool on her part. It stung anyway. In a perfect world, he would have time to help her out of the fix she presently found herself in. Normally, he would have the luxury of being seen out and about. He would have moved in and out of circles without anyone connecting the dots to her, and he would probably even have been able to have a conversation with her mother without the senator being any the wiser. Bringing in his family wouldn't work. Harding was too busy with his new fiancée, and Barrett wouldn't feel right putting anyone else in danger anyways, so it wasn't like he could ask him.

In fact, Barrett couldn't contact anyone who could assist Connie without them having questions about where he'd gone. Reaching out to any of his co-workers would only serve to put them in danger.

Helpless didn't begin to describe how he felt as they walked out of the hotel room and into the hallway.

"There's an exit down this way," he said, motioning toward the intersection at the elevator bank. "It'll help us avoid the front desk."

He kept his chin to his chest as they walked, making it impossible for security cameras to make out his face.

Connie did the same, hiding much of her figure by pressing up against him. His arm was around her shoulders, and he couldn't help but think being with her like this was the most natural thing.

All of his protective instincts flared as they stepped out of the building. Now that he knew her, and he felt like he'd gotten to know the real her this afternoon, the thought of anything happening to her burned him from the inside out.

Not his problem, though. He had enough trouble on his heels without adding to it. Her tagging along would only slow him down. He needed to remind himself of the fact every few minutes because his emotions were trying to take the wheel. They wanted her right next to him where he could make sure she was safe. They wanted to bend his head down a little further and claim those cherry lips. They wanted to wake up tomorrow morning in a tangle of legs and sheets with her right by his side.

The best way to describe his out-of-control feelings was like a puppy on steroids: adorable to look at from a distance but could destroy a house if left unattended for longer than five minutes. Making love to Connie would cause just as much devastation. He needed to remind himself of the fact because his heart got heavier in his chest with every step toward the Chevy.

"Nice ride," she whispered as he walked her to the passenger side.

"I'd planned to fix it up someday," he said. "New parts. Fresh paint. Give her a facelift."

"Why? I like the paint just like it is. It looks worn in like a favorite chair," she said with true admiration in her voice. "Besides, what's so great about things being new? They don't make anything like they used to. Things cost a lot of money and still break. If you ask me, the older, the better."

"I'll take your opinion under consideration," he said, surprised by her passion as he opened the door for her.

"See," she said as it squeaked. "All these little imperfections give the Chevy so much character. All the cars pretty much look the same now. This beauty is one of a kind."

He couldn't agree more as his gaze roamed over the creamy skin of her face but had a feeling they weren't thinking about the same thing any longer.

———

Connie had two thoughts after realizing she'd probably just come very close to death, prior to Barrett showing up the other night. One had to do with her mother. How would she survive after losing both of her children? It had been twenty years since Mitchel's death and her mother never fully recovered. Would Connie's death be the final straw? There'd been signs of her mother making progress in recent years: picking up with a few of her friendships from college; going out to lunches that weren't required by her husband's job; and every once in a while, a spark lit up otherwise weary green eyes.

The second was personal. After growing up around a manipulative stepfather, Connie realized that she'd never truly allowed herself to trust a member of the opposite sex. Hunter Owens III had put the nail in the coffin when it came to being able to open up to others. Living like a bug underneath a glass, Connie had had to limit her friendships, until even those eventually petered out. The man's claws had been and still were in every part of her life.

Going away to college had been a godsend. She'd met and dated Ryan Binninger. The crush she'd had felt like true love at the time. Looking back, it was a serious infatuation, one she'd believed was reciprocated. The first night he'd slept over, one of her stepfather's guards had banged on the door at three o'clock in the morning. Ryan had freaked out, thinking this was some kind of police raid for the two of them losing their virginities. The whole situation had been mortifying. This was also the first time she'd realized her stepfather's eyes would always be on her.

The sun was behind them as Barrett navigated east on the farm road, leading to her vehicle. She thought about the folks hunting her but couldn't imagine who would have a person like Barrett on the run. He most likely wouldn't give her so much as a hint, but she decided to ask anyway.

"How bad is the guy chasing you?" she asked, unsure if Barrett would even respond. The conversation always seemed to get derailed when it came time to talk about him.

"Worst nightmare material," Barrett said, surprising her with a response.

"Do you still work in law enforcement?" she asked, figuring she might be able to capitalize on the moment.

"Yes," he admitted. "But I'm on leave at the moment."

"For how long?" she continued.

"As long as it takes," he said and then clamped his mouth closed. His gaze intensified on the stretch of road in front of them and it was clear this conversation was over, but he'd given her something to remember him by. Though forgetting Barrett would be an impossible proposition either way. For someone she'd known for only a couple of days, and had been asleep for most of that time, she felt a connection like she'd never experienced before. She chalked it up to two strangers facing uphill climbs and nothing more, because a real and lasting connection with a stranger made no sense with her history.

His gaze narrowed as it swept the area, side to side to well beyond the road. He seemed to be clicking into investigator mode now, quiet and focused. At least he knew what to look out for and had the training to back it up, whereas she was in figure-it-out-as-she-went mode. The main thing she had going for her was the years she'd talked her stepfather into allowing her to take martial arts. If Connie had known just how much she would need those classes later, she would have worked even harder. The lessons had been an outlet for her during her high school years. She'd been able to sell her stepfather on the idea, telling him that she wanted to be ready for college and the day she didn't have personal security around. Little did she know she would need to hire her own bodyguards against the man who'd adopted her.

Connie scanned the area. There was nothing but a two-lane farm road, field, and a whole mess of mesquite trees out here. Another thought struck. What if the person she'd been running from had taken pictures of her? They could be posted online right now and she wouldn't know any different. She'd had to ditch her cell phone after she realized how easy it was to track her with it.

"I just had a dark thought," she said, breaking into the silence. "My face might already be all over the news."

"There wasn't anything about you the last time I checked, late this morning," he said.

"You checked to see if I made the news?" she asked.

He shook his head, and it dawned on her that he must be watching the news to see if the person who was after him ended up caught. It was the only thing that made sense. An active law enforcement officer going off the grid; it wouldn't happen for no reason. It also occurred to her the reason he seemed so insistent on the two of them parting ways might have to do with the fact Barrett questioned his abilities against his target. This must be one bad dude for a person like Barrett to be intimidated.

"Does any of this look familiar?" he asked as he slowed the Chevy.

"No. I've got nothing," she admitted. Her headache had morphed into a dull ache right between her eyes, but there was some relief. At least the sun was to their backs. She couldn't imagine driving right into it. Putting on sunglasses had helped too.

It was strange to think she'd been here the night before last, considering none of this terrain seemed remotely familiar. How had she managed to drive? How had she picked this road? And where was she heading?

"I just realized something," she said. "I don't have th key fob."

"It's inside your purse," he confirmed. "I placed it there after moving your SUV."

The fog in her brain blocked out recent events, no doubt from the trauma. Another question practically smacked her in the face. Was someone expecting her? Without her cell phone, there was no way for anyone to get into contact with her.

Barrett slowed the Chevy before making a clunky U-turn. She realized he passed up the spot where he'd tucked her vehicle, wondering if he'd done it to ensure he'd found the right spot or make certain no one had followed them.

There was nothing and no one on this stretch of road. It was the kind of area folks might assume a tumbleweed would roll across the street. There had to be deer and most likely plenty of wildlife, considering the nearest town was at least half an hour away.

Connie had been lost in her thoughts for most of the drive here. Barrett pulled over to the side of the road and cut off the engine. He reached into a bag and then strapped on a holster. Despite being from Texas, she had very little knowledge about handguns. She was more familiar with a shotgun.

Opening the door and stepping out of the Chevy, the sobering reality she faced struck like a physical blow. Stomach bile burned the back of her throat as she searched for her small SUV. A glimmer of silver paint sparkled from in between the trees when she really looked at it. Finding this exact spot after dark would have been next to impossible.

Reaching inside her purse before palming her key fob, she took in a breath. Granted, being with someone who had her back for a change was a welcomed development. She couldn't remember the last time that had happened. Walking away from Barrett was proving harder than she imagined it would be.

Fine. Connie had a one hundred percent track record of dealing with difficult days. This one was right up there, but she could handle it. Rather than give some long, drawn-out goodbye, she wished him luck and then faced her SUV. The fact he followed meant she wasn't in the clear when it came to Barrett yet. Water pooled in her eyes as she kept her focus forward. At some point in her life, she would like to be able to slow down and trust the world around her. She would like to just be, without expectations or camera lenses trained on her as she walked out of a grocery store or down the street.

"Duck," was all Barrett said as they reached the tree line. A second later, the crack of a bullet split the air from somewhere to the right of her. In the next instant, Barrett's heft knocked her to the ground and then covered her. "Be as still as you can."

Connie's vehicle was ten feet in front of her and yet she couldn't seem to reach it.

CHAPTER FIVE

White hot pain shot through Barrett's right shoulder. He risked a glance and immediately saw the red dot spreading on his shirt. He released a string of curse words that would have made his grandmother blush if she was still alive.

Whoever was after Connie had found her vehicle. Could he protect her long enough to get back to the Chevy? Splitting up seemed like a bad idea in hindsight. But then, he couldn't have known someone would be waiting here.

The marksman had been patient too. He'd made certain they were far away from the Chevy and not close enough to the SUV for cover. He scanned the area in the direction the bullet had come from but didn't see anyone. A sniper?

How would Hunter Owens III explain his only daughter being shot and killed with a high-powered rifle? How did the man intend to explain it to his wife?

Or did he have the woman convinced Connie was headed down a path of drug and alcohol use?

"I need to get a visual on the shooter," he whispered to Connie. "Can you keep an eye out for anyone else in the area?"

"Yes," she reassured.

The scrub brush was tall enough to cover them, but they needed to move now that the shooter knew their location. All he had to do was correct his aim another couple of inches and he would deliver a devastating shot. Out here, with the wind blowing and the sun in the shooter's eyes, it would take someone who knew exactly what they were doing to pull off a hit at this distance. Still, Barrett wasn't taking any chances.

Dirty Joe wouldn't be as sophisticated or indirect as this. In fact, Barrett figured Joe would want to be a whole lot more personal when he attempted to kill Barrett. Revenge killings were usually up close, involving something more intimate than a long-range rifle with a scope. A stabbing or strangling would be more his speed. And dirt. He'd want to be close enough to use his trademark move on Barrett.

"Call out what you see, when you see it, okay," he said to her.

"Got it," she reassured. Despite a calm voice, he could feel her body trembling beneath his.

"On three," he whispered as he studied the direction the bullet came from. "One. Two. Three."

He popped up and fired a warning shot toward the east. Whoever was out there did a good job of hiding. Then again, the person had had a day and a half to prepare for this moment. Enough time to ensure the shooter blended into the background. Now, he was leaning toward someone who'd worked in Special Forces. Would Hunter Owens III have the kind of resources to employ someone from Spec Ops? The short answer was yes.

"Next time, I want you to make a run for the SUV," he said, lowering his head down.

"Not without you," she said.

"I'll provide cover for us both," he said. He had no plans to leave her to her own devices out here.

"I have the key fob. I can sound the alarm if you think it'll help," she said.

"Good thinking. I'll take any distraction that I can get," he stated, and meant it. A single second in a situation like this could mean the difference between life and death. "At least try to make it to the tree line. It'll be harder to get off a clean shot there."

"Ready?" she asked.

"Whenever you are," he stated. With a little luck, they'd both make it into the SUV.

"And...*now*," she said, a second before the alarm blared.

Barrett helped her scramble to her feet and covered her as she bolted toward the tree line. A couple of steps in and she turned to him. He fired off a shot.

"Come on," she urged.

The minute he realized she waited for him, he made a beeline toward the SUV. The bullet should give them a couple of extra seconds. They made it without incident, but it was too early to sigh relief. Connie made it to the SUV as Barrett went back against a nearby tree trunk. At this point, he ascertained there was one person out there. There'd only been activity from the original shooter's location so far. No sign of a second shooter. One to one odds were better than average for Barrett.

Barrett climbed into the backseat not a minute after Connie claimed the driver's side.

"Can you get us to the road?" he asked.

"No promises, but I can try," she said, as she started the engine.

He didn't want her to panic and feared she might if she realized that he'd been hit. First things first, they needed to get out of immediate danger while he stemmed the bleeding and assessed the damage. It was too late to go back to their hotel room and they needed to move on from here anyway.

"I have something in my backpack to create a smoke screen around us, if you're comfortable leaving your vehicle here and taking the Chevy," he said. For better or worse, she was stuck with him for the foreseeable future.

"Okay," she said, and he could tell based on the monotone quality in her voice that she was in shock. Civilians weren't used to being shot at. Barrett's job brought him face-to-face with plenty of folks who'd rather kill him than spend the rest of their lives in jail, so he had the training and experience to move past his fears and force a smile when he looked in the face of danger. Anything less would make him unfit for his duties.

Barrett quick-checked his shoulder and decided, for better or worse, he could live with bleeding until he could get them far away from there. Every bounce and jerk of the SUV as it traversed over scrub brush made his blood pulse a little faster, but the injury wasn't life-threatening just as he'd initially suspected.

Connie whipped the SUV onto the roadway with a jolt before pulling in front of the Chevy and stopping. "What now?"

"Cut off the engine and get ready to bolt," he said as he located a smoke bomb can inside his backpack. He cracked the door, pulled the ring, and then tossed the soup-sized can toward the general area of the shooter. "Also, bring your shirt up over your nose and mouth if at all possible. Breathe in as little smoke as you can."

She nodded as she cut the engine off.

"Grab whatever you need from here," he said.

"Most of my stuff is still in the Chevy," she pointed out. It was a good thing they'd decided to bring her SUV to the Chevy before unloading. As much as he hated to admit it, the Chevy was going to have to go at some point. It was too distinct, and the person who was after Connie knew what it looked like now.

"Let's go," he said as a gray-black smokescreen emerged.

He moved quickly into the driver's seat as Connie claimed the passenger side. Seatbelt locked, he immediately started the engine and navigated onto the farm road and around the SUV.

Connie gasped.

"You're bleeding," she said with panic in her tone.

"It's not as bad as it looks," he reassured.

"What can I do?" she asked, as a motorcycle came into view behind them.

"Stay low until I get us out of here," he said, staring into the rearview mirror.

She seemed to catch on quickly after turning around. "Give me the Glock."

"Are you familiar with guns?" he asked.

"Not really, but you are right here and you can walk me through it," she stated, a sudden calm overtaking her. Some people freaked out in the face of an emergency; some people curled into a ball and froze; others were able to dig deep and rise to the occasion. Connie seemed to fall into the latter camp.

"Underneath my seat," he said as he watched the helmeted rider, dressed in all black, roar toward them.

Connie located his weapon before cranking down the passenger side window. "Give me a clear shot and I'll see what I can do to blow out his tire."

"Unlock the safety mechanism, aim, and shoot," he said. Barrett cut the wheel left, into oncoming traffic as the sun's glow practically burned his retinas. He put a hand up to shield his eyes as Connie followed his instructions.

She got off a shot. Whether she hit the motorcycle or not didn't matter at the moment, because the rider veered enough to end up in scrub brush. Head over heels, he flew off the bike.

"Call 911," he said.

"Will it be traced back to your phone?" she asked.

"This is an encrypted burn phone," he stated. "It's expressly made for this purpose."

"When we stop for the day, I expect a full explanation as to why you seem a little too prepared for exactly this kind of scenario," she said in a tone that left no room for doubt.

If they were going to spend time together, she deserved to know what she was getting herself into. After what they'd been through together, it seemed wrong to split up. But was it safe?

———

Connie had called for an EMT and explained the person who'd been in an accident was armed and dangerous as they fled the scene. She immediately hung up before the call could be traced, despite Barrett's assertion that the line was encrypted.

Scooting over on the bench seat, she turned sideways to focus on his shoulder. Next, she grabbed the emergency medical supply pack that Barrett had made for her back at the hotel, and went to work on his right shoulder. His shirt was soaked with blood by this point and she could only hope it looked worse than it was in reality. She rolled up the sleeve over his shoulder as he pushed the Chevy as fast as he could.

There was a lot of blood, but her fear that she would be facing a geyser was eased. She grabbed gauze and pressed it against the wound. Thankfully, there didn't seem to be a bullet in there.

"Sorry," she said as Barrett grunted.

"No problem," he immediately said, putting her at ease. This had to hurt but he was letting her know that he could handle the pain.

"Can you lift your arm a bit?" she asked.

He nodded and she helped by cupping his elbow in

her hand. She brought her knee up so he could rest his elbow on top while she grabbed medical tape. She opened the package and then taped up his arm over the gauze, so it would stay in place. The wound was low on his shoulder, so that made it easier to secure.

"Where do we go from here?" she asked after putting away the supplies and scooting back over to her side of the seat. She buckled up, then turned to him. His coloring was still good, so she took that as a good sign the wound was superficial. He might need stitches or at the very least a butterfly bandage. They could take a more serious look once they stopped for the night. Her stomach growled and her headache returned with force, but none of those things mattered right now.

"Away from here," he said.

Since that was as obvious as the nose on her face, she figured he didn't have a set plan. Or maybe he didn't want to tell her.

"I was on my way to a fishing cabin that no one knows about, save for me and a couple members of my family. I doubt any of them remember the place because no one has talked about it in years," he said. "It won't be much—I can promise you that—but it'll provide shelter from the chill in the air and any storms we might encounter. It's off the grid, so there's no cell phone reception. We'll be away from any news."

"You're waiting for him to get caught, aren't you?" she asked. "The man you're running from."

"That's right," he said, without hesitation. His openness surprised her. "He's dangerous and I had to disappear so he wouldn't use my family or anyone I care about against me."

"Otherwise, you would have stayed?" she asked.

"Something like that," he said. "I had to draw him away from Austin."

"And your family," she stated.

"That's right," he confirmed.

"Does this mean you'll take me with you?" she asked.

"Yes," he said.

"Good," she said. "And when this is said and done, I never want to see another gun in my life."

He didn't take to her comment, as evidenced by the way his expression soured.

"If you ask me, you have a hidden talent. Maybe you should consider taking a few gun classes so you can get more comfortable with one," he said. "Not many folks could make a shot like you just did."

"Beginner's luck," she said, wishing she could repress her daddy issues that she thought were gone until they'd resurfaced now. Her stepfather had been the one to take her out on their property in Crickett, Texas, and force her to learn to shoot. In a strange way, she had him to thank for being able to flee the motorcycle. It would have been faster than the Chevy and would have caught them in no time. The driver probably had a plan for shooting them in the back or coming up to the side and taking them both out with one shot. If he hadn't been the one responsible for her near-death experience, she'd have been inclined to thank him. If he had it his way, she'd be dead already, another casualty in the war against drugs—drugs she never took. Connie rarely even drank, save for the occasional social gathering where she would nurse a glass of wine for the entire evening so she could have something to hold onto. Plus, hosts always seem to want their guests to constantly have a drink in hand.

Ignoring her daddy issues wasn't the same as dealing with them, she was learning the hard way. It had just become so easy to turn a blind eye to the situation at home in favor of living her own life. And it would have been so much easier to convince her mother to leave her husband if she got angry instead of depressed. Her mother had played right into the man's hands by becoming another victim.

"Even so, it was impressive," he said with a touch of awe in his voice that filled her with pride.

"What's your last name?" she asked, figuring she might as well go for broke. When he didn't respond, she added, "We're going to be spending twenty-four-seven around each other for the foreseeable future. You saved my life because, clearly, I would have been found by the time the drugs had worn off, and traveling with you now, I'm putting my life in your hands again. I'm trusting you; you should trust me too."

"Quinn," he stated quietly.

"As in *the* cattle ranching Quinn family?" she asked, incredulous. They were one of the wealthiest families in Texas and had been a financial target of her stepfather for campaign money. She was one hundred percent certain she'd heard the name thrown around over the years. "Your family contributes a lot of money to politicians."

"Wouldn't surprise me," he said. "But you're thinking of the other side of my family. My cousins are the cattle ranchers. This side of the family has more public servants."

"Oh, interesting," she said. "What branch do you work in?"

"I have a feeling you figured me out back at the hotel," he admitted, slowing down to the speed limit as he checked his rearview mirrors.

"Law enforcement has a certain swagger when they walk," she said. "It's impossible to get rid of it completely, and I could tell you were someone who was used to wearing a gun by the way you keep your elbow away from your hip. That could mean private security, which I ruled out because a for-hire security person would have most likely left me where I was the other night."

"Have you ever considered working in law enforcement?" he asked with a Cheshire cat grin.

"Never," she said emphatically. "Not after what I've seen them do, after swearing to protect and serve."

CHAPTER SIX

"Not everyone is willing to compromise their morals," Barrett defended. He wasn't sure why it was suddenly so important to him that Connie knew about all the honorable men and women in law enforcement. Normally, he left people to their own opinions. This felt different. For reasons he didn't want to examine, he needed her to know how many good people there were in the world.

And, she was right; there were jerks and crooks in every profession, no matter how hard law enforcement officials worked to weed them out. And just like weeds in a garden, they threatened to choke out all the good. He, for one, would never allow that to happen on his watch and being powerless to change other people's minds was enough to give him a headache. The bigger war was for another time. With Connie's slight nod, he seemed to have won a small victory. If he had to change minds one at a time, so be it.

"I'm a U.S. Marshal, by the way," he finally decided

to come clean. Why not? Connie was right. The two of them were going to be holed up together for heaven knew how long, and it seemed silly to keep secrets between them after what they'd been through just now. "A man I locked away two years ago who swore revenge has escaped prison and was last seen heading my way."

"Don't you get threats all the time?" she asked.

"Yes, ma'am. I do," he admitted, figuring it was also part of the job.

"Why is this one different? If he's coming for you, I would think that would make your peers rally around you so you guys could arrest him again," she said. Her logic wasn't flawed.

"Normally, that's exactly what we would do," he stated. "But this guy is different. His name is Dirty Joe and—"

"Oh. He's notorious," she said in a hushed tone as though saying the words too loudly would cause him to appear. Dirty Joe wasn't Beetlejuice, and Barrett had no qualms about speaking the man's name out loud.

"That's right," he continued before she could get too worked up. "Which is the reason I decided to enact the plan."

"I overheard a couple of cops on their lunch breaks talking and laughing about their own 'plan'. I thought it was a joke," she said.

"No, ma'am," he said. "Yes, we all joke about it, but most everyone I know has thought seriously about what they would do in a situation like mine."

"This fishing cabin," she hedged. "Will it be safe?"

"Should be," he said. "No one in my family has been out here since I was a kid, that I know of. I'm about one hundred percent certain folks have forgotten it existed."

"How so?" She tilted her head to one side.

"I read somewhere that your family owns land in Crickett," he recalled.

"That's right. It's our family retreat. I spent a whole lot of summers there," she said.

"Does your family own other properties?" he continued.

"Well, yes, now that I think about it. We own a little place in Galveston on Jamaica Beach, and I overheard my stepfather talking about a hunting lease in the past," she said.

"I'd bet money your stepfather owns land in various parts of Texas," he said.

"Never mind," she said. "I see your point. So, this fishing cabin...how rustic is it?"

"There's indoor plumbing," he offered. "One bathroom though, and since I haven't been out here in years, I have no idea what shape the place is in."

"As long as no one can find us there, we'll make do," she said with a lot of hope and little conviction in her voice. "It's a little hard to be picky right now."

"True enough," he agreed.

"How much longer until we get there?" she asked.

"A couple more hours," he stated.

"We should probably stop off before then and redress your wound. It looks like the bleeding has stopped, but we'll want to do a better job if you're going to stave off infection," she said. Her stomach growled and he realized she was probably starving. Now that his adrenaline had faded, he could admit to needing a bite to eat. The power bar and fruit he'd eaten at the hotel had been enough to stop him from wanting to chew his own arm off. That was about it. The effects of hunger were starting to take hold.

He glanced at the rearview mirror to ensure no one was following them. They got lucky since the emergency vehicles had to have come from the opposite way. There weren't a whole lot of options out here when it came to roads, which also meant fewer escape routes. He was painfully aware of the fact at the moment.

Now that Barrett planned to bring Connie along, the risk multiplied tenfold. Not only did she have a corrupt politician for a father seeking her out, but they had all his considerable resources in the mix.

Barrett smiled at the thought as Connie curled up in the seat next to him, resting her head in his lap. He'd learned a long time ago that when faced with danger, he could fold up the tent or smile. He chose the latter. *Hold onto your horses, cowboys, it just got that much more interesting.*

It was impossible to view having Connie by his side as a bad thing, though it definitely complicated things. Hells bells, he hadn't been real sure earlier how he was going to be able to drive away after dropping her off at her vehicle. This just made the decision a whole lot easier for him.

Cutting her loose and sending her out into the wild on her own seemed like the cruelest thing he could do to a person. All he had to do now was come up with a new plan. In the day and a half that she'd been asleep, he'd convinced himself this was all going to be as easy as dropping her off at her vehicle, and then him turning the tables on Dirty Joe. Barrett was not a deer loose in the woods with a dozen hunters; he was a fighter and had no plans to make this easy on Dirty Joe.

Connie closed her eyes as he searched for a good place to stop off. A few thoughts cycled through his mind. Could the SUV be traced back to Connie? Would local law enforcement make the connection to the motorcycle rider and the vehicle now parked on the side of the road? Barrett didn't want to disturb her rest with too many questions right now. He would stop as soon as he could find a safe place to pull over and deal with his right shoulder.

Now, he knew what his brother felt like. Harding, also a U.S. Marshal, had been shot while tracking down a felon. He'd been nicked on his side and had a bruised rib, but had also met the love of his life while in the hospital.

Harding had hired the nurse on duty to stay with him for a couple of days at his home, and ended up with a fiancée out of the deal. Finding Naomi had been the only bright spot in what could only be described as a horrific situation. His brother wouldn't be back on the job for weeks while he healed, despite itching to go back to work within days of going home from the hospital. Harding had taken the shooting hard even though he would never admit it to Barrett. Now, he knew exactly what it was like to be hit—and it was just as frustrating and awful as he'd imagined it would be.

While Barrett was looking for a good spot, he reconsidered whether or not he needed to ditch the Chevy. The motorcycle guy now knew what Barrett drove, and that would make them a much easier target.

After the crash, the guy should be headed toward the hospital. There was little chance he'd walked away from a wreck that sent him flying over the handlebars at the speeds they were going, let alone make a phone call to someone else to pick up where he left off. Driving around in a blood-soaked shirt would definitely send up a red flag to anyone who pulled them over. Not to mention convince the cops and everyone else they came across that they were, in fact, connected to the motorcycle incident.

Which brought him back to his first point. Did he really have to ditch the Chevy? The vehicle was meant to be unique, because it drew attention to it and not the driver. Most fugitives drove white or silver sedans and turned right at every light they encountered when fleeing a scene, because they couldn't risk waiting around for the light to turn green or to get an arrow so they could go left. There weren't exactly any lights out here. This stretch of road was typical of Texas, flat and straight. This made it easier to see what was coming, but harder to hide. It was probably only a matter of time before law enforcement drove this way, looking for the reason the motorcycle had flipped. On the off chance the rider was conscious, he could give up Barrett and Connie by making up a lie about them.

The rider had no idea that Barrett was a U.S. Marshal. Then again, his career would be in serious trouble if he was caught looking like this, and wrapped up in an attempted murder case while he was supposed to be taking a couple days of leave. He could only hope none of that would happen. He couldn't be linked to Connie, considering the two had barely met.

Finding a new vehicle would prove tricky. Getting a new ride wasn't the worst of ideas, but how? He had no contingency plan for that. He was supposed to already be at the cabin, and he was on going on a wing and a prayer at this point anyway. There was no way to get a rental, and besides, what were the odds of a car rental place being out here in the boondocks anyway? Slim to none.

Calling one of his brothers for a drop would be a last resort. If he could avoid involving them any more than they already were by being related to him, he would. The problem with the Chevy was that it made him memorable. So, with a blood-stained shirt and a girl, he was basically an advertisement for trouble.

Barrett came up on an intersection and a four-way stop. A sign for the town of Moody Creek, with an arrow right, meant at least a little bit of civilization. He took a left instead, figuring law enforcement would go right. Besides, at this time of evening there weren't any other vehicles on the road. It wasn't a shock to him since he grew up in Gunner. The same was true of most small towns in Texas, especially when it got the slightest bit chilly outside. Summers saw a bit more action, but nothing compared to a city like Austin that seemed to never sleep. College kids walked around twenty-four-seven, and there was constant traffic on the roads. He preferred the liveliness of the city to the quiet country-side despite loving the land with his soul.

After driving a few minutes on the gravel road, he pulled over, figuring this was as good a place as any to fix himself up. He needed another power bar too; the last one had worn off a while back and his stomach was starting to remind him a little more regularly than he'd hoped. Plus, Connie was hungry.

The minute the engine cut off, she pushed up to sitting. Her movement was slow and he could tell she'd actually fallen asleep.

"Where are we?" she asked.

"Your guess is as good as mine," he admitted. "I took a side road, so I could do something about my shoulder."

"I can't believe I fell asleep," she said. "How long was I out?"

"Not long," he clarified.

"I didn't mean to," she said, biting back a yawn. "Now that I'm awake, what can I do to help?"

"Eat something," he said as he reached for a sack. Bad move considering he was right-handed. He issued a grunt.

"I'll get it. What am I looking for?" she asked.

"The power bars and fruit," he said, trying to roll his shoulder and getting nothing but stabbing pain with each attempt.

"It's worse than we realized back there, isn't it?" she asked, producing two bars. She opened them both and handed one over with a bottle of water.

"Nothing more than a flesh wound," he said, dismissing the notion it could be worse. He didn't want to go to the mental place where he needed stitches or a trip to the ER. That would be the equivalent of a red flag waving over both of their heads. Since the adrenaline boosts had faded and the injury was still fresh, this was the worst of it.

The light from the phone app was enough to see her eyes rolling.

"Hey, tough guy, it's okay if it hurts," she said. "I can't imagine what it must be feeling like."

"The throbbing is the worst," he admitted with a grin. "I can feel my heartbeat in the wound."

"That's awful," she said with so much compassion in her eyes that he almost forgot about the pain. Almost. The heartbeat thing was real, and the throbbing was no fun at all. But staring at her like he was right now, reality had a way of fading into the background. The coil in his chest tightened, begging for a release only she could give.

"I'll be good to go after a couple of ibuprofen," he said, shoving those thoughts aside. It took an intense amount of effort to look away, but at least his pulse relaxed a little bit when he did. "I was waiting to get to the cabin first. Figure this is nothing a good night of sleep won't cure, or at the very least make feel better."

Connie polished off the power bar before handing out apples next. She used one of the empty bags as a makeshift trashcan once they'd eaten down to the cores. She opened her own bottle of water and finished it within a matter of seconds. Then, she retrieved a second bottle and scooted closer to Barrett. The emergency medical kit now sat in between them and her serious expression signaled it was time to get down to business as she turned on the interior light.

Gingerly, she removed the tape and gauze. It had done the trick as far as stopping the bleeding but she'd been right earlier when she said they needed to do something before infection set in. Her fingers grazed his skin—skin that burned underneath her touch, causing wildfires to light inside him.

"This might hurt but I have to clean it out and see what we're really dealing with here," she said. "Take off your shirt."

"Not until you take me out to dinner," he quipped before letting a slow smile overtake his lips. He shrugged out of the shirt but not without pain.

Connie laughed and it was the most musical sound. And, yes, he was going all-in by being sappy. Being around her had a way of softening him and causing him to notice those little things about her. Things that probably flew right past him on other dates. This, however, was not a date. He should probably remind himself of the fact. They weren't here for social hour, as evidenced by the sheer amount of pain shooting through his shoulder as she poured water over the exact spot where the bullet had grazed.

"Sorry," she said, wincing and then making eye contact like she was making sure it was all right to keep going.

Barrett clenched his back teeth until he thought his jaw might crack. He gave a slight nod.

Suck it up, buttercup. His new mantra definitely applied to this situation.

"I'll be quick," Connie said as she blotted the area with fresh gauze.

"You're doing fine," he reassured.

"Okay, that's good to know because I feel like I'm killing you," she said, before compressing her lips and applying antibiotic ointment to a fresh piece of gauze. She gently pressed the gauze against the wound before applying fresh tape. Her eyes lit up when she said, "All done."

And then, out of nowhere, she leaned toward him and pressed her lips to his. His shoulder might hurt right now but his heart was going to do a real number on him when this ordeal was over. The instant she kissed him, he was in deep. Thunder boomed in his ears and stray lightning struck the center of his chest as she teased his tongue inside her mouth. This would be the benchmark for all future kisses, and he knew right then everyone else would come up short.

CHAPTER SEVEN

The kiss was supposed to be the equivalent of a peck on the cheek. At least, that was the lie Connie had told herself. Her lips seemed to have a mind of their own, and they'd sought the comfort of Barrett's. For a split second, he tensed and she feared he might stop her. It didn't take long for him to relax as he brought his hand up to cup her face and draw her closer to him.

The simmering heat between them turned up a couple of notches and her breath quickened along with his. This was the first real indication that he was having the same physical reaction as her, and the knowledge only stoked the fire.

Barrett pulled back first.

"Believe me when I say that I could stay here longer than I care to admit with you just like this," he said, and he was almost as winded as her. "But we should go."

"Do you want me to drive?" she asked, willing her own pulse to slow to normal. She should probably be embarrassed, and yet she couldn't bring herself to regret the best kiss she'd ever experienced, bar none. Barrett was compassionate, intelligent, kind, and beyond gorgeous. He would laugh at being called that, but that didn't change the facts. His feet were firmly planted on the ground, and yet he managed to still be sexy as all get-out. Her heart was in trouble and her brain decided to pick that moment to point out just how much this man could shatter her.

"I got this," he said, breaking into the thought before it could take hold. "If you want to lie down again, the motorcycle rider would tell the law to look for a couple if he was able to talk, which I doubt. Still, it might not be bad for them to only see one person in this vehicle. Plus, I've thought about it six ways past Tuesday and realized there's no way to change out the Chevy. Not legally anyway."

"To be honest, I wondered how you would pull it off," she stated, thankful to be able to shelve the out-of-control attraction to him for now. "I knew it was on your mind."

"What about your SUV?" he asked, getting back into his seatbelt after putting on a clean shirt and then starting the engine again. "Can it be traced back to you?"

"Nope," she said with a smile. "But it can be linked back to the senator. It's one of his personal vehicles and doesn't belong to one of my friends like I said before. The man never gets rid of anything. He kept it on the property in Crickett, so I borrowed it when I realized things were heating up. I couldn't very well use my own car. The men doing his bidding would absolutely know to look for my convertible. I had to try to throw them off the trail somehow."

The way he smiled, like he was proud of her, sent more of that campfire warmth swirling through her. Barrett Quinn was dangerous to her heart, and she couldn't care less right now. He was also keeping her alive and protected. The latter was a feeling she reminded herself not to get used to.

As Barrett navigated back onto a gravel road, she curled on her side and rested her head in his lap again. The next time Connie sat up, he was parked and cutting off the engine. She must have dozed off again, because it felt like no time had passed in between the stop to care for his shoulder and parking in front of the cabin.

It was literally black as pitch outside. From the headlights, she could see that there were plenty of trees surrounding the small, isolated cabin. This was probably a strategic pick on Barrett's part, because he'd already said trees made a shot harder to nail. In the event bullets flew, they had a better chance of getting away in a thicket.

Barrett wasn't kidding when he said the cabin was remote and rustic. It was one story and couldn't be much more than one long room. A spider web so big, so thick that it was probably sturdy enough for her to climb caught her eye. Her body involuntarily shivered at the thought of the size of spider required to build that.

"This time of year, there's not much threat of rattlers being on the porch," Barrett stated.

"I grew up in Texas and spent many summers in

Crickett, but there was always staff there—and, believe me, I know how that sounds, but that's the life of a politician's daughter—so, what I'm saying is that I never saw spiders," she said involuntarily shivering again.

"Never?" he asked in a tone of voice that almost made her laugh out loud.

In fact, she did laugh because the alternative was to cry to relieve some of the stress of recent events.

"I was more the stay on the porch and drink ice tea type, growing up," she admitted.

"I'm guessing spending your summer in Crickett wasn't exactly your idea," he said.

"To be honest, I didn't mind it so much when my brother was alive," she said, realizing that this was the most she'd talked about her brother in decades. It was nice and a way to keep his memory alive. "There was a basketball halfcourt right by the house and, of course, a swimming pool. Those were the only two places my brother could convince me to go."

"A city girl," he said.

"Through and through," she said. "Except, of course, horses. I grew up riding and loved them. I would have spent the whole day in the barn if the senator would have let me. I wasn't really allowed to hang out in the barn, because my stepfather didn't want me around all the hired hands."

"Sounds like a restrictive childhood," he said.

"You have no idea," she said. "I think there were just always eyes on me. He made certain of that. Even when I left the house there was always someone ready to tattle to him. The senator was a powerful man and folks seemed to care more about impressing him than being genuinely my friends."

"Prom?" he asked.

"Had to be home by midnight," she said. "And had to take one of his bodyguards with me, who drove us and pretty much kept a visual on me the entire night."

"Sounds awful," he said.

"I can imagine that sounds like quite the opposite of how you grew up," she said. "Plus, I always had food to eat and clothes on my back. There's no need for a pity party when there are folks out there who don't have enough money to put food on the table."

He nodded.

"What was your childhood like?" she asked.

"Let's head inside, clean the place up, and I'll tell you all about it," he said.

She'd noticed that Barrett had a way of changing the subject when it came time to talk about his background. Granted, they did need to get inside now that they'd pulled up to the cabin.

"Word of warning," he said with a half-smile, "I have an idea what we're about to walk into and apologize in advance that it cannot possibly be up to your standard."

"My new standard is finding shelter and staying alive," she said. "I have no other standards at this point."

"Those I can meet," he said. He reached for the Glock and pressed it into the palm of her hand. "Why don't you stay here and give me five to ten minutes to see what we're dealing with, clean up, and clear out the cobwebs."

"I'd rather come inside with you, if that's okay," she

stated. The spiders were nothing compared to the horrors of the reality they faced.

Barrett came around to the passenger side after taking back his weapon. He opened the door for Connie. He linked their fingers after he helped her out of the vehicle. Normally, she would be fine on her own. However, this whole situation had her knocked off balance. She would take all the comfort she could get at this point. Their hands clasped together was her link to reality. The connection grounded her in ways she didn't really want to explore or explain. And even the jolt of electricity was comforting.

"Not sure if I mentioned this yet, but there's no electricity inside the cabin," Barrett said.

The chill in the air promised it would be a cold night. Without heat, she figured she could pile on clothing and figure out a way to make do.

"We'll figure it out," she said. "Worst case scenario, we put on a bunch of layers and huddle together on one of the beds."

The gentle squeeze of his hand sent another rocket of warmth through her. At the very least, they could use the heat between them to stay warm. Believe her when she said there was plenty of fire to go around when she stood anywhere near him. The thought of lying skin-to-skin, curled up against Barrett's rock-hard body, sent more warmth through her than if she'd been standing in the July midday sun. It also sent a trill of awareness skittering across her skin. Then again, she'd had two brushes with death in the past couple of days. Her body's reaction had to be intensified because of recent events. It was near impossible to believe that this is

what she should have been expecting from past relationships.

––––––

Barrett wasn't kidding about the rustic nature of the
cabin or the size. He was scratching his head at how he
and his four siblings ever fit in here at one time. The
place was essentially one long rectangle with two sets
of bunkbeds to one side of the room, a fireplace along
the wall leading to the kitchen, a bathroom, and something most folks would call a kitchenette. He had no
idea how anyone would be able to cook a decent meal
in there, and yet he didn't remember it being a
problem the few times he'd come out here when he
was just a kid. Of course, a campfire was the preferred
method of boiling water, cooking, and so on. And then
there were roasted marshmallows at night, again on the
campfire and not in the kitchenette. This wasn't much
more than a two-burner hotplate and an oversized
cooler.

Camping supplies were stacked in a closet that, once
he opened it, resembled a half played Jenga game. He
feared pulling out the wrong piece because the rest
might come tumbling down. Whoever stacked this
seemed to be in a hurry, which also made sense that it
was done by him and his brothers. They'd had the
patience of a two-year-old standing in front of a tub of
ice cream with no parental supervision back then.

Gas lamps hung at various intervals on the walls.
And, based on the flashlight app on his phone, a thick
layer of dust covered the flooring.

"Bottom or top?" he asked Connie, as he studied her face in the glow of the app.

"Bottom might be warmer," she said, reasonably.

"Okay," he said. "It'll just take a few minutes for me to clean this up, if you want to put on coffee."

"Coffee?" Her eyebrows drew together in confusion. "I didn't think there was electricity here."

"Gas should work. It's all butane, but you raise a good point as to whether or not everything is filled. If memory serves and it still happens, we have a caretaker who stops by a couple of times a year. Or at least we used to. You and I will have to double-check for ourselves to see if everything's good to go," he said.

Barrett went to the kitchen drawer and pulled out a few boxes of matches. He handed out a couple to her. "I'm sure you had much fancier lighting in Cricket, but this will keep us out of the dark."

"Perfect to me," she said, and he didn't want to admit how much that comment warmed his heart. There was something very primal inside him that made him want to make her life more comfortable while the two of them were together. They may have come from opposite worlds, but in this moment at least, they seemed to be meeting in the middle.

Connie's next few moves were as impressive as she was. She immediately went to work figuring out the gas lamps, getting them lit while he brought in supplies from the Chevy, then pulled the sheets off furniture to reveal relics from a different time.

"At least we have running water," she said, as she turned on the spigot over the kitchen sink. Connie also did something he least expected someone from her privileged upbringing to do...grabbed a broom and started sweeping. She located a mop next, before getting down on hands and knees to reach underneath the beds. There was a whole lot more impressive about Connie Owens that Barrett didn't think it was a good idea to think too much about before spending a night together in the same bed.

"It's supposed to get cold tonight and I apologize in advance for not being able to use the fireplace," he said.

"Not a problem. We'll figure out how to stay warm," she said without hesitation. Had he totally underestimated this princess?

He almost laughed out loud at the thought. She might be a city girl, but she was a far cry from a pampered princess. In fact, the way she was scrubbing the countertops right now, you'd think she'd done it her entire life, rather than relied on housekeepers.

"I thought you grew up with maids," he said. "How is it you know how to do that so well?"

"One could say the same thing about you, Quinn," she quipped. Yes, they were famous in Texas for having money.

"Touché," he said, even more impressed with her quick wit now that she was conscious and talking. He had learned a great deal about her and her family situation. His heart went out to her after losing a sibling at such a young age. Don't even get him started on the calloused response from her stepfather. Barrett might not be close to his father, but the man would be devastated if anything happened to one of his sons. To prove the point, he'd been the first to call around to the family when Harding had been shot and hospitalized.

Just thinking about her loss made him want to call up his brothers and tell them that he loved them. Funny how easy it was to take family for granted when they'd always been there for you when you needed them. Everyone on his side of the family did their own thing, and he could admit to being a little bit jealous that his cousins were all back on the ranch together, working side-by-side, continuing to build their father's legacy. His uncle might have been a jerk for most of his life, but he'd done something right in his seven sons. Uncle T.J. wasn't the one responsible for bringing them up. That had been Marianne's doing. She was the family's housekeeper growing up and was now married to the patriarch. Not only that, but she was also a good person. So much so, Barrett wasn't real sure Uncle T.J. deserved her. Marianne had been a mother to Barrett's side of the family as well. The marriage of her and his uncle had thrown everyone for a loop, but only because they'd been secret about their relationship. And, to be honest, no one believed Uncle T.J. had enough brains in his head to marry someone who was clearly right for him and such a good person. His dating history had left a lot to be desired before Marianne.

All of this made Barrett think that he should reach out to his brothers and see about getting together at least on a monthly basis. It would be tricky to coordinate everyone's schedules since the five of them worked in various branches of law enforcement and had very different days off. Surely they could figure out a way, once a month, to spend a day together. They could even rent a lake house and meet up there. Or, he was certain Quinnland would welcome them with open arms. The thought of being with all of his brothers and cousins caused an unexpected wave of emotion to crash down on him.

Barrett really had gotten good at compartmental-izing his life and emotions, ignoring anything that had the potential to make him sad. Being with Connie was the first time he'd actually wanted to feel something. The thought struck like stray lightning on a sunny day.

Connie stood up straight, put a hand on her back, and stretched.

"There," she said with a whole puffed-out chest full of pride. "Now, I can make coffee. And by the way, I haven't lived with a maid since I went to college. Growing up in the senator's house, I was never to make my own bed or fix a meal. And while that probably sounded like heaven to most people, growing up, it never taught me how to take care of myself for the day I lived on my own." She issued a sharp sigh. "Then again, I was supposed to marry Mr. Right and have kids by now, instead of living on my own and working as a patient advocate in a children's hospital."

"Sounds like a job the senator would approve of," he said. "I can already see the headlines for his do-good daughter. He'd be sure the reporter mentioned what a great parent he'd been to have such a lovely daughter who was dedicating herself to advocating for children."

She rolled her eyes and laughed. "He thinks I live off a trust fund," she said. "There's no way I'm telling him that I have a real job."

"Ever?" he asked.

"I'm required to go 'there' for occasional family dinners, but I never talk about what I really do for a living. As far as he knows, I'm trying to get my internet jewelry business off the ground."

Well, Barrett really laughed now. The animated way in which she spoke got him.

"How on earth did you pull the wool over his eyes on that one?" he asked.

"You'd be surprised how quickly his eyes glaze over when I go into the details of beading and color palettes…" She laughed a genuine laugh that seemed to roll up and out, filling the room with imaginary bubbles and lightness. It looked good on her, that moment of joy, and he hoped to be around to see more of it.

"You're better at this cloak and dagger thing than I gave you credit for," he teased.

"When you grow up in a house of lies, you learn some survival skills," she said.

"You never have to lie to me," he said, surprising himself with the comment. He just needed her to know that she could tell him anything. He seemed to surprise her too, as her eyes widened for a split second.

"I know," she said in a barely audible tone. There was something about that musical voice that rolled over him and through him, making him believe things would somehow work out.

Barrett would describe the next couple of actions he was debating as not the brightest. When Connie lifted her gaze to meet his, he should have looked away. Didn't. But should have nonetheless. In fact, instead of doing anything that would break the moment happening between them, he leaned into it. He took the couple of steps closing the distance between them. He searched her eyes, making sure that he was welcome.

Her tongue slicked across her bottom lip, and he should have looked away from that too. Didn't. And at least in this moment, he didn't have it inside him to regret his actions.

And he probably should have stopped her from taking that final step that would put them within inches of each other, where an insane heat welled up in the space between them. Didn't. Instead, he brought his hands up to rest on her shoulders, allowing his thumbs to graze the creamy skin of her jawline as she tilted her face up toward his.

Barrett couldn't bring himself to regret dipping his head down and claiming those cherry lips of hers, no matter how much it complicated the situation. And it did, because it made this dangerous situation even more personal. He should be walking away from Connie; she had enough going on without adding Dirty Joe into the equation. The criminal would use any means to get at Barrett, including torturing and murdering anyone Barrett cared about. He did care about Connie. His feelings toward her grew exponentially the more they talked. Not only was she intelligent and beautiful, but she had a kind heart. She'd loved her brother beyond words, and was willing to put herself in harm's way to protect her mother while figuring out how to bring her stepfather down. The easiest thing to do would be to go directly to the media with the proof she had against the senator. She refused until she was able to get her mother out of the situation. All of this while not certain her mother would be willing to walk away. Connie was putting her life on the line to give her mother a choice.

Connie parted her lips and teased his tongue inside

her mouth causing literal fireworks to go off inside his chest. It didn't take much imagination to realize how amazing sex would be with her. This woman was capable of rocking his world both in and out of the bedroom. Could his heart take losing her, though?

CHAPTER EIGHT

Connie brought her hands up to Barrett's shoulders to anchor herself. As it was, her world had tilted on its axis and it was all she could do to stand upright. The second she felt Barrett's muscles tense under her grip, reality slammed into her and she realized her mistake.

"I'm sorry," she said, not meaning to hurt him. The last thing she wanted to do was cause him any more pain, so she pulled back and tried to catch her breath. There was something about kissing Barrett that hadn't happened in any other kiss she'd experienced. Barrett had set a new bar when it came to lips touching, and it was one she was pretty certain he was going to hold the record for the rest of her life. "You should get some sleep."

Through labored breaths, Barrett's face muscles tensed like he was about to put up an argument. He seemed to think better of it when he issued a sharp sigh and said, "You're probably right. We should be okay here for a few hours at least. It's supposed to dip close to freezing tonight, and again, I apologize in advance for not being able to use the fireplace. The lights are risky enough."

"Won't someone know we're here based on the Chevy?" she asked.

"You are absolutely right about that, and I had planned to move it by now," he said. "I know a spot a little ways up where it'll be out of sight and safe."

The thought of him leaving her alone in this cabin, even for a couple of moments, sent an icy chill down her back. She had bigger fears than spiders when it came to being by herself, thanks to her stepfather. She could only hope the motorcycle rider was the last of the senator's minions to be sent that day. Knowing him, there would be others. Relentless was a good word to use in describing her stepfather. Other 'r' words followed, like ruthless and rich. Those three words were a bad combination in the same sentence. She closed and locked the door behind Barrett, half of her wishing she could go with him, the other half realizing it would be best for her to stay put and find blankets. Once the lights went out in the cabin, it would probably feel even colder.

She eyed the set of twin bunk beds and realized someone of Barrett's size would never fit on a twin bed with another person. With no source of heat other than blankets and each other, sleeping separately seemed like a bad idea.

The frames could be pushed together to create one big bed. Connie walked over to the nightstand in between, and then moved it out of the way. She managed to pull one bunkbed toward the center of the small room, then went to work on the next.

Pleased with herself, she capitalized on that win by searching in a tall dresser with deep drawers. She opened the bottom drawer and...bingo! She located two thick blankets that she immediately spread out. Staying busy kept her nerves a notch below panic while she waited for Barrett's return. Their kisses still sizzled on her lips, despite the fact getting into a romantic relationship with Barrett would be worse than a bad idea. This whole situation, their time together, was temporary at best.

Strange how empty the place felt without him here. She figured it was more than just his considerable size. There was something about the man that filled the room, *every* room. Under different circumstances she would like to get to know him better. Connie almost laughed out loud. Their worlds never would have collided in the real world. Period. She was certain of the fact, considering she kept such a low profile. When she really thought about it, she wondered if she was truly living at all.

She'd seen peeks here and there of a sense of humor with Barrett. Turned out he could be a funny person. It would be nice to get to know him better under different circumstances, even though the two of them came from totally different worlds. *But did they?* A little voice in the back of her mind questioned. He wouldn't belong in her world even though it was a world she'd like nothing more than to escape.

What was taking Barrett so long?

Coffee sounded like a really good idea, except that

they'd both been through an exhausting couple of days and they needed rest. If she stayed up, she had a feeling Barrett would too. Of the two of them, he was in more immediate need of sleep. At least she'd been able to grab a couple of minutes here and there on the way to the cabin. Plus, there was that whole day and a half conked out, even though she still felt like she could sleep for a week and still not be caught up.

At least she had a roof over her head and was out of the wind that had been picking up speed along the drive. Her thoughts drifted back to the couple of kisses they'd shared. The memory burned into her body and mind. Just thinking about them caused her breathing to quicken and her pulse to race.

Then again, that was Barrett Quinn. It would be a very long time before she would encounter another man like him.

The wind was picking up speed. At times, it howled so loudly that she felt like she was in a twisted version of *Wizard of Oz*. She reminded herself to breathe and that Barrett was a very capable person. He would be fine. She didn't want to start panicking or worrying about him, even if she felt herself doing it anyway.

The doorhandle jiggled. The sound of the key being inserted was the first wave of relief. The second came when she saw Barrett's face as he entered. He quickly closed and locked the door behind him, a stark reminder of the dangers they faced.

Connie probably should have been getting ready for bed. However, she was finding it difficult to think straight after those kisses. Plus, she wanted to be prepared to bolt, just in case Barrett didn't come back.

The thought threatened to suck all of the air out of the room.

He is here, she reminded herself. The thought of doing any of this on her own was too much and she sensed he felt the same. The bond between them caused her to feel like she knew him intimately, which should be strange. The twenty-four hours she'd been on the run alone had been the loneliest of her life. Then there was her cell phone. The problem with constant connectivity was that once it was gone and she could no longer reach out to people she knew at any moment, she felt alone in the world.

It was strange, really, because she didn't exactly have a long list of friends. It was just mostly her and the few co-workers she went out to lunch with on occasion.

Most of her life had been spent on her own, especially once Mitchel had died. She gave her head a shake to stop the tears that were welling in her eyes. This wasn't the time to go there about missing her baby brother, even though the floodgates had finally opened now that she had someone to talk about him with.

"We should freshen up and get to bed," she said to Barrett to resist the urge to run over to him and bury her head in his chest. He was strong and a very large part of her wanted to lean into his strength.

He nodded and there was a mix of emotion behind his eyes. This seemed like a good time to walk away and brush her teeth in the sink. She located her overnight bag and freshened up. Her jogging suit could double as pajamas. They would help keep her warm. And, probably most importantly, reduce any temptation to get closer to Barrett than she needed to be. As it was, their bodies would be pressed against each other, seeking warmth.

A sensual skitter raced across her skin just thinking about it. This seemed like a good time to redirect her thoughts as she washed her face before bed.

Barrett did the same as she slid into the sheets first. The covers were heavy and would provide a decent amount of warmth.

"I hope you don't mind that I pushed the beds together," she said. "I figured we could stay much warmer if we huddled together."

"Good idea," he said as he followed her. "We won't freeze like this."

In fact, the bed was quite warm once he got inside. He eased onto his back, then she curled into the crook of his good arm. Once again, the world righted itself and she felt like she was right where she belonged. Connie chalked it up to recent events, but she couldn't think of a place she'd rather be right now. Here, with Barrett, she felt safe and secure, which nothing about their current situation should give her that sense.

"Can you sleep?" she asked.

"Not right away," he said.

"We could talk a little bit more," she suggested. Tomorrow, the reality of her situation would hit with the force of a two-by-four. She was going to have to figure out a way to get to her mother without giving herself away. Oh, and by the way, she was going to have to figure out a way to do all that without the senator or his henchmen finding her first. "But only if you want to."

"I'd like that a lot actually," he said. "Tell me about what you were like as a kid."

"Shy," she admitted and could feel her cheeks burn. "My earliest memory of elementary school came with me, telling my best friend Annabella Spencer about how much I hated going to Crickett and leaving my friends behind for the whole summer. Annabella must have mentioned something to her parents, who, in turn, mentioned it to others. Eventually word got back to the senator. I was sent to bed without supper after a good butt-chewing. The next morning when I woke up, I had to kneel in the kitchen for an hour before I was allowed to eat. My brother was just a little kid at the time and he tried to give me some of his food. I told him not to and he got in so much trouble." She blinked back tears. "I felt responsible for him and got so angry with my friend and her parents. I made a pact right then and there never to tell any of my secrets again. In my young mind, I decided that anything I said would end up used against me and hurt my baby brother in the long run."

Connie felt Barrett's arm tighten around her. He didn't immediately speak.

"The senator sounds like a class-A bastard," he said. The words came out in a low, throaty growl. Connie would hate to be on the wrong side of the person capable of making it feel like thunder clapped inside the room just by the sound of his voice. Except this was Barrett, and she knew that he would never unleash his temper on someone he loved. He had the kind of honor that would keep him from metering his own justice. But make no mistake about it, he would see to it that justice would be served.

"After, the only person I confided in was Mitchel," she said. Losing him meant not only losing her best friend, but her only confidant. "I also realized that if I gave too big of a show of emotion, there would be consequences."

As there would be with Barrett, but nothing like the meanness and punishment from the senator. The consequences of falling for Barrett were far deeper on the inside. And yet she couldn't regret doing just that... falling for him. Not now. Not in this moment when she finally felt like she could talk to someone. Even if it meant shattering her heart later. And it would.

Barrett reached for Connie's hand before lacing their fingers. He brought hers up to his lips, where he feathered kisses across her skin. It would be so easy to get lost with her right now and forget the outside world. But keeping a clear mind would ensure their safety, so he forced thoughts of how right she felt curled up against him out of his mind. He stopped his free hand from roaming across her silky skin as he'd listened. Very few people had ever touched his heart in the same way as Connie. In fact, he could count on one finger the number of people who had. Her.

And that number included all of his past relationships. He'd never once considered being in a serious relationship, let alone seen himself falling in love. His life was takeout for one, and he liked it best that way. Sharing space with another person hadn't been on his radar, not to mention in his heart. Was he single? Not really. He'd been in a steady relationship with freedom until now. One that had been working well until Connie came along and made him want things he'd never envisioned for himself.

Her steady, even breathing said she'd fallen asleep in his arms. Man, how he wished he could keep her there for days, protect her. Of course, doing the latter meant eventually getting out of bed and leaving the cabin. He had no idea how well he'd be able to sleep with the wind gusting to the point the cabin shook, but he knew that he needed to try. At the very least, lying still and closing his eyes would come in a close second to actual REM sleep.

Thoughts swirled around, hammering his skull. In a perfect world, he would be able to call Harding to bounce ideas around. Then again, in that perfect world, he wouldn't have been shot in the shoulder. He and his brother had that in common, even though Harding had taken a bullet to the ribcage. Being away from his cell phone was actually testing his patience to no end. It was silly how much he'd come to depend on his technology. Working in law enforcement didn't help. His service vehicle had a laptop mounted from the dashboard. So, that wasn't helping with his technology dependency.

As a kid, he would have laughed if someone had told him a device would feel more like an appendage. He hadn't even watched TV until he got old enough to go to the movies in town on a date, and he wasn't sure if that even counted. He'd grown up outdoors and with as much freedom as he could handle. His upbringing was a sharp contrast to Connie's. His heart went out to her for growing up like a bug trapped underneath a jar. As much as he prized his independence, that would have driven him out of his mind.

Connie was hands down one of the strongest people he'd ever known. She deserved a life where she didn't have to hide. The question was, how to give it to her while keeping out of sight with Dirty Joe on the loose. Barrett was out of ideas. Running had seemed like the right play in the heat of the moment. He couldn't regret meeting Connie along the way. But what now?

Hide out until her father's henchmen found them? Wait until Dirty Joe tracked Barrett down?

It was a tempting thought to chuck both of their lives and hideaway in this cabin while closing out the world. As amazing as that sounded, they both had lives and responsibilities to get back to. And now that Barrett had enacted the plan, he realized it was only one of those things that sounded good in theory. In practice, not so much. The truth of the matter was that he would rather die while facing his enemy than being shot from behind as he ran away.

The bottom line was he needed to come up with a Plan B. The thought carried him off to a fitful sleep.

A gust of wind rocked the cabin, causing Barrett's eyes to fly open. Rain pelted the roof. Based on the sound, the droplets were Texas-sized.

"How long have you been awake?" Connie asked, stretching and yawning at the same time. His arm had gone to sleep at some point through the night, but he hadn't wanted to wake her when she looked so peaceful. At least one of them should get sleep, and he'd gotten enough rest to get by on.

"Not long," he said. "In fact, I was happy as a bug in a rug until the wind and rain woke me."

"What time is it?" she asked, and her sleepy voice was sexy as all get-out. Everything about this beauty made him want things he knew better than to want.

"Half past nine," he said. "The rain is making it seem like it's still the middle of the night."

She pushed to sitting. The movement caused him to wince, and she turned to him with large doe-eyes.

"What can I do?" she asked.

"Give me minute," he reassured. "I'll be fine."

"How is that even possible?" she asked.

"I grew up with four brothers and seven male cousins," he said on a laugh.

"That would do it," she said, smiling. Don't even get him started on her smile—a smile that caused the coil to tighten in his chest and the birds to sing. "I'll put on coffee."

Connie practically bounded out of bed. She was already brushing her teeth before he could sit upright without feeling light-headed. Lack of movement over the past few hours caused the discomfort, he decided, shaking out his left arm to get the blood moving again.

By the time he joined her in the kitchen and brushed his own teeth, she'd figured out coffee. He took a sip from the mug she'd handed over.

"Not bad for a first attempt," he said with appreciation.

"It's not awful," she conceded. "This seems like a real good time to be grateful that I'm not one of those mocha-frappe-sugar-overload coffee drinkers."

He laughed at the description, thinking he'd probably said something very similar in the past.

"What are the chances that we can get to Wi-Fi and I can check my e-mail?" she asked, staring up at him with those honey-brown eyes that made him want to say yes to anything she asked.

"We'd have to drive into town, which isn't terribly far," he said. "Might not be awful to see if we can grab hot food while we're there. And ice for the cooler along with food supplies. It wouldn't hurt to be able to cook here for a couple of days."

He wasn't quite ready to spring the news on her that he had to figure out the timing on facing down Dirty Joe. She deserved to know what he was up against and that he intended to take the man down again.

"Tell me something that I don't already know about you," she said, catching him off guard with the sudden change in topic. She'd been biting down on her bottom lip—a sure sign she was trying to figure out whether she should speak her mind—so he probably should have seen this coming. If they were going to spend time together, she deserved to know what he was up against.

Where should he start?

CHAPTER NINE

"Picking up where we left off, I'm on paid leave from my job," Barrett said after retrieving the Chevy. They had already polished off a couple more power bars that tasted more like dirt than food and tended to each other's wounds. Thankfully, Connie's headache had subsided and she could see the end of it nearing. There was just a bit of residual pain at the spot right between the eyes. She could deal with it.

"To get far away from the criminal you locked behind bars," she said, going ahead and finishing the thought for him as she clicked her seatbelt on. She already knew this much and that was about the extent of her knowledge.

"Dirty Joe was nicknamed for the fact he stuffs dirt in his victims' mouths and noses," he explained.

"Does he do this after their dead?" she asked, mortified.

"Sometimes," he admitted as he navigated onto the gravel road leading away from the cabin.

"Well, I realized as soon as I asked the question that it doesn't really matter. Dead is dead," she said while trying to shake off the imagery.

"In a manner of speaking, that's true," he continued. "But one is far worse than the other to the person who is still alive."

Her body involuntarily shivered at the thought. He made a good point, though. That ranked right up there with being buried alive in her book. Both made her cringe.

"Before I tracked him down and arrested him, he'd been in custody once before. A pair of competent agents were transporting him and he managed to kill them both with no weapons other than his bare hands," he said as he kept his gaze on the road. "By the time I got to him in the jungle, I'd learned everything there was to know about the man. Once there, I studied his movements, his habits. I knew when he worked out, when he ate, and when he slept. Most importantly, though, I knew when he went to the restroom and that he made the walk by himself. Other than then, he always had a couple of his lieutenants with him. Once I spotted his vulnerable spot, I watched some more to make sure he didn't waver. He didn't. When I took him down, the arrest was easy. Almost too easy. But then I guess he was already calculating his next moves. He was playing a chess game five moves ahead of me," he said. "Sure, he'd been caught for the time being..."

"...but then he found a way to escape," she said.

"During his arrest, he detailed out the ways in which he planned to hunt me down and kill me," he stated. "Let's just say the man had...*has*...some creative plans."

"I'm guessing they involve dirt in some way," she said, wondering why he was telling her this now when he'd been so quiet about himself and what he was up to before.

"You catch on fast," he said with a half-smile.

"I'm guessing working in a dangerous job nets quite a few threats like these," she said, noticing how easy he seemed to be able to talk about this now.

"Yes," he admitted. Any trace of a smile was now gone.

"So much so, that you'd get used to them," she continued, realizing this one must have really hit home, considering the man had killed not just one but two U.S. Marshals, and at the same time no less.

"They do come in on a regular basis," he admitted. "And, no, I don't take most of them seriously. The biggest danger in my job has usually already happened by the time the perp is in cuffs. I've immobilized him or her and the hard work is behind me. None of the felons that I've arrested have been happy to see me or be arrested by me. So, yes, they generally make a few veiled threats or try to strike a deal. Those are always fun."

"I bet they can get really creative," she said, thinking pretty much everything would be on the table for someone who regularly broke the law. Women? Check. Money? Check. Drugs? Check.

"You would be surprised at what I've been offered," he said. "A guy once asked if he could trade his wife for his freedom. Said I could have her for a month."

Connie laughed at that one and it was a nice break in the tension. "I wouldn't want to be sitting on the couch, watching TV when she arrived back home from essentially being prostituted out."

Barrett shook his head.

"Her biceps were bigger than mine," he said, laughing. "And his. I highly doubt she was the type to go along with a scheme like that. Folks get desperate and sometimes start throwing everything out there, along with the kitchen sink. In fact, one guy who owned a contracting business to launder his drug money through actually did try to throw in a kitchen sink."

"I hope it came with a complete remodel," she said, thinking people could be funny when they wanted to be. Of course, she'd always kept her nose clean, having learned early on the senator was always watching. But, honestly, she would have been the squeaky clean type anyway.

Barrett's laugh was one of the best sounds she'd ever heard. She liked the way it seemed to roll up from deep in his chest. She liked the sound it made. And she liked the way it made her feel when she heard it. Barrett's insanely good looks were only part of the story when it came to his magnetism. He had a physical presence that made it known when he walked into a room. He was smart and kind. Very few people got it all, and by all she meant good looks, intelligence, sex appeal, and a sense of humor. The man had a body that was made for sinning and his lips held more temptation than ice cream on a hundred-degree day. Add his honesty, gorgeous face, and honor to the mix and he was irresistible. The senator would despise a man like Barrett.

"Why are you telling me about Dirty Joe now?" she

asked, circling the conversation back to the beginning. "What does it mean?"

"I just thought you had a right to know what I'm up against," he conceded.

"Does that mean you plan to drop me off somewhere?" she asked. "Because between the two of us, we have several would-be assassins on our tails."

"Double the danger," he said. "And each would come at us from a different angle. But that's not the biggest risk here."

"Then you'll have to fill me in because I can't think of anything riskier," she said, drawing on a blank on how this situation could be worse.

"Dirty Joe would use you against me," he informed.

"But we barely know each other," she defended even though she felt quite the opposite, like they'd known each other half their lives. It was probably because she'd confided more in him than in anyone since before her brother's death when they were kids. As an adult, no one had come close.

"He doesn't know that," Barrett stated.

"We can tell him. Claim that I was just a hitchhiker that you picked up alongside the road," she offered, figuring they could sell the lie if need be, mainly because it wasn't too far from the truth. Her thumb might not have been sticking out as she stood on the side of the road but that didn't mean Barrett hadn't rescued her. Without him, she would be dead. Period.

"There's no way he would believe that I picked up a random, beautiful woman on the side of the street. Plus, all he'll have to do is take one look at me and he'll see right through the lie. He'll see that I care about what happens to you," he said with the kind of honesty that drew her even closer to the fire—a fire that would burn her in the end when they went back to their normal lives.

Barrett had made a point, though.

"What should we do about it?" she asked, resigned to the fact he was going to tell her where and when he was planning to drop her off or put her back on a bus home.

"I can't hide from him, waiting around and jumping at every noise like someone who should be afraid of his own shadow," he said following a thoughtful pause. "I've always been one to face my problems. This hiding will drive me insane."

Connie didn't offer a response. She understood a person like Barrett, who was used to tracking down criminals and not being the one hunted, couldn't stand to hide out in a cabin for long.

He pulled into a gas station off the side of the road, the first indication civilization was near after spending the night in the cabin. If she were pressed, she would have to admit being in the cabin felt better than rejoining people, even though she still hated spiders and creepy-crawlies.

Her change of heart had everything to do with the company and nothing to do with the conditions. Those were sparse.

"You can check your e-mail on my tablet," Barrett said, retrieving one from the floorboard underneath the driver's seat. He kept a weapon in there too.

"I'd also like to see if I'm on the news," she said, wondering if she'd gotten away before the person who'd drugged her and put makeup and tight clothes had taken pictures. Discrediting her would make anything she said less believable, even with proof. Politicians were a little too good at spinning the truth for their own benefit, no matter who else it hurt.

"Let's hope you got away beforehand," Barrett stated. He would know the kind of damage those pictures could do to her reputation and how much they could discredit her.

He handed over the tablet once he'd switched it on and entered his password. "Here you go."

She cocked her head to one side.

"Honestly, I'm surprised you even brought this with you," she said. "Isn't this a way to track you?"

"If anyone tries to trace the location of this tablet, they'll end up on a wild goose chase to Minnesota," he said with that trademark grin that was so good at lowering her defenses.

"That's good to hear," she said.

"I never used it personally," he said with a little spark of pride in his voice. "It was packed away to be used with the plan."

"Here goes nothing." Connie took the offering with a sharp sigh. She pulled up Austin-American Statesman, figuring it was as good a place as any to start her search. Nothing was what she found.

"That's a good sign," Barrett said when she showed him the screen.

"Let's try Google now," she said. The most recent story about her was from Fathers' Day, when she'd been forced to meet her parents for dinner and a photo op. "This is really good news. Unless the person who has the pictures intends to use them as blackmail."

"They might try your e-mail if that's the case," he offered.

"Right," she agreed, figuring the same. There was no way to reach her using her phone, and the person with the pictures—if there even were any—would probably realize the cell was the first thing she would have ditched. She pulled up her personal e-mail. "Very few people know about this account."

There weren't any unknown names in her inbox, so she checked the spam folder. Nothing in there as long as she didn't count all the 'banks' holding money in a foreign account for her or all the 'single' females in search of sex-only with no strings attached. She rolled her eyes at those as relief washed over her. This could mean there were no pictures.

The e-mail in her inbox that caught her attention was from her mother. There was no subject, so she almost didn't click on it, worried it might be a scam.

I don't know where you are and I can't reach you on your cell. Come home immediately. Your father says you're in danger. Please. Come home, Con! Let me know that you're alive.

"She hasn't called me that since my brother was alive," Connie admitted to Barrett as her heart battered the inside of her ribcage. It was one of the many sweet things about their relationship that seemed to have been swept away in her mother's grief. "I thought she'd forgotten all about it."

"Can you trust the e-mail actually came from her?" he asked. The question was a legitimate one.

"I believe so," she said.

"The senator might be manipulating her," he pointed out.

"True," she admitted. "I guess we're just going to have to step out on faith at some point. How much longer can I run without getting caught anyway? Especially once you drop me off."

"Is that what you think?" he asked. The hurt in his voice convinced made her think twice.

"Wasn't that your intention?" she asked as the first seeds of hope took root that she'd misread the situation.

"I can do whatever you want," he said, and there was a coldness to his voice that put a chill in the air.

Had he just closed off? Put a wall up? Because last night couldn't have been more intimate than if they'd actually made love, and she hated the thought of breaking their connection.

———

Two targets who would soon be on the road home. Barrett questioned his judgment about sticking together when they probably had a better chance if they split up. But, no, he hadn't intended to leave Connie stranded, any more than he could walk away from any friend in trouble. Or at least that was the lie he tried to tell himself, to tone down some of his out-of-control feelings toward the senator's daughter. Focus would keep them alive. They would have time to sort out what they meant to each other later. All he could allow himself to focus on now was keeping her alive and arresting Dirty Joe.

"I'd like to stay with you, but I also realize you have your own priorities right now," she said with a tightness to her voice that he hadn't heard from her before. He couldn't tell if she was hurt or angry.

"I only have one priority, aside from helping you," he pointed out because he didn't want to make this situation out to be worse than it was. Besides, he knew her better now. He could hear the loneliness in her voice when she talked about her family. She was all alone in the world and he could hardly fathom what that might be like; he'd grown up surrounded by family. So much so, he could probably have been better off without a Quinn at every turn. Yet, he couldn't imagine going through life without his brothers or cousins. The thought of Connie doing all this alone brought out all of his protective instincts.

Going back to Austin was the right move, even though it was also the riskiest. The e-mail from Connie's mother could be a fake. Her mother's account could have been skillfully hacked or, heck, the senator could have logged onto her account instead of his.

"We can grab something to eat, gas up the Chevy, and then head to the cabin to pack up," he said. And he hoped they wouldn't pay dearly for their next move.

CHAPTER TEN

A warm meal, a full tank, and a packed cabin were boxes Connie could check off as she stood outside on the porch. She'd never been much for nature but was starting to regret that. Being forced to go to Crickett every summer, especially after Mitchel was gone, probably had a lot to do with the reason she usually couldn't stand being outdoors. But this area was peaceful and beautiful. She could see herself spending time here relaxing. A peace like she'd never known filled her in those few seconds, as she allowed herself to stand there and breathe in the crisp, fresh air.

"The Chevy is packed up," Barrett's deep baritone washed over her and through her. The man's voice was sex in a bucket. It was so easy to lean into her attraction to him and so dangerous to even think about right now, let alone try to act on. And even though her heart wanted to trust him, her logical mind said it was only a matter of time before she would retreat.

"Guess we should head out then," she said, wishing

she could stand here just a little longer in this magical moment.

Barrett came up from behind her and looped his arms around her. She leaned back, feeling a wall of muscle, despite skin that she remembered as soft. He was silk over steel and she could stand like this all day. His heart beat a strong, steady rhythm.

"Is it wrong that I wish we could just stay?" she asked, only half-kidding. Facing the task ahead meant one or both of them might not come out alive. Their enemies were dangerous and excelled at committing crimes. There were no guarantees.

A twig snapped to their left and she almost jumped out of her skin. Barrett's arms tightened around her, reassuring her as he whispered, "It's just a rabbit."

The other side to the coin—and there always was one—was that sticking in one spot made them sitting ducks.

With a deep breath in and then out, she managed to step away from Barrett and toward the vehicle. The cabin had been good to her, giving her a night of rest she wouldn't have had otherwise.

Connie felt Barrett's presence behind her as she walked to the Chevy. She realized that she'd forgotten to check for a news story on the motorcycle rider. If anything serious had happened to him, or he'd died, there most likely would have been a writeup. A hospital stay might not get the same attention but it was possible.

"How many hospitals do you think there are in the area?" she asked Barrett as she rounded the back of the vehicle to the passenger side.

"Probably just one." Barrett claimed the driver's seat and then buckled up before starting the engine. He backed out of the hidden spot, then navigated onto the gravel road.

"What do you think about stopping by on our way out of town?" she asked, thinking any information they could get about the shooter would be welcomed.

"I wish it could be that easy," he said. "I'm afraid the sheriff or his deputy put together the intention of the rider. The guy was traveling with a high-power rifle near an abandoned vehicle that is registered to an invisible person."

"What if we just showed up and pretended to be visiting someone in labor and delivery? We could pretend to get lost and look around," she said. The idea of leaving the area without knowing what had happened to the rider, when they could possibly talk to him and get information, sat hard in her stomach.

"This isn't Austin," he warned. "We would stick out like a sore thumb and I can't risk him having a buddy who might recognize us and pick up our trail. My main mission for the day is to get you back to Austin in one piece and it's risky enough driving the Chevy, but I can't think of a better solution since neither one of us can rent a vehicle in our real names."

"Once we get close to home, I can get us into something else," she responded. There were a couple of vehicles she had access to.

"Do I want to ask how?" He sounded skeptical, and he was probably right. Her plan was to drive home in one of the senator's vehicles.

"The best way for me to get to my mother is to drive in something familiar to everyone," she said.

"I'm not sure that will work either," he said. "Won't everyone be looking for you now that you've disappeared?"

"On a small scale, yes. I know that I can't go to my apartment," she said. "Have we figured out where it's safe yet?"

"Not mine either." He immediately nixed the thought and she figured as much. Any place linked to either of their names would most likely be watched.

"Do you think Dirty Joe will be working alone?" she asked. Facing a double threat meant they needed to be twice as prepared.

"This is personal. He wants the credit and he wants to make a statement with me," Barrett confided. He was in the best position to understand the inner workings of the kind of mind who would think nothing of killing two U.S. Marshals, let alone a third. The two he'd murdered were keeping him in custody. They hadn't even been the ones to arrest him.

Someone like Dirty Joe sounded like the type who would hold a grudge.

"Where did you arrest him?" she asked. It might be a clue to where the man might end up. "In Texas?"

"Oh, no," he said with a headshake. "I tracked him down in a South American jungle."

"Why wouldn't he just go back there?" she asked.

"He can't until he can hold his head up high. To him, that means taking down the person who one-upped him," he said. "Otherwise, he'll look weak to the men who follow him. If that happens, any one of them could challenge his leadership and take over the operation. He's already been gone for months. To restore his reputation as top dog, he needs a big win. I'm a big prize."

"All you were trying to do was arrest a criminal who belongs behind bars," she said.

"He doesn't see it the same way," he said as the half grin returned. She'd noticed he always seemed to smile whenever the subject of being in real danger came up. Was that how he did his job?

She admired his stubbornness. Not many people could look at danger and smile. She'd always had enormous respect for those who served their communities despite the possible personal cost. Their sacrifices were honorable.

"It's an awful way to think, but it does make sense," she conceded. "If he was a good man, he wouldn't need to be in handcuffs."

"Back to the motorcycle rider," he circled the conversation around to where they'd started. "Are you good with staying on the road instead of trying to stop by or call?"

"You made a lot of sense there too," she said, circling back to the e-mail from her mother. At least, she hoped it was from her mother. There were so many other possibilities, like she was being led to slaughter. If only there was a way to get a message to her mother beforehand to investigate. "I just wish this was easier somehow and I'm even more worried about my mother after receiving that e-mail from her. *If* it even is from her."

"Would the senator remember the special nickname?" he asked.

"I don't think so, but the man is a brilliant strategist and knows how to use people's weaknesses against them," she said in truth. It sickened her to think about him that way, especially since her mother still lived with the jerk.

"Is there any chance the senator is monitoring your mother's e-mail?" he asked. "There are programs that can easily be installed to search for keywords, etcetera."

"What you're saying is that even if my mother did write the e-mail, my stepfather could very well know I'm likely on my way home," she said, knowing it sounded exactly like something Hunter Owens would do. After watching him use her brother's death for political gain, she wouldn't put anything past him. The only tears he'd shed were in public. "When my brother died and my mom could barely get out of bed, I went to check on her one morning. *He* was standing over the bed, with his hands in the air, yelling at her to get up and do her duty. That was all he cared about after she lost her only son, was that she go to a fundraiser luncheon for his political campaign."

"The senator sounds worse than some of the scum I lock behind bars, if you ask me," Barrett said.

"He abuses his power," she said. "There isn't much difference between him and Dirty Joe, except that my stepfather gets away with it."

"He won't," Barrett reassured. "We won't allow it."

"How do you plan to take down a man as powerful as him?" she asked. "I had a plan before, but I can see all the holes in it now. I don't have a chance against him and neither does my mother. Maybe that's the reason she gave up on life in the first place. Maybe she folded in the tent when she realized what a monster he was."

"We'll figure out a way to help her get out of the situation if she wants out," he stated. "I've seen more domestic abuse situations than I care to in my line of work, and you'd be surprised at how many women want to stay with these men."

"I guess they're just resigned at some point," she said. "Broken."

He nodded. "We can offer help until the cows come home, but it's up to her to take it," he said. "Which doesn't mean we won't give it everything we have to convince her to leave and help her find a better path."

He sounded so confident they were going to get out of this alive and in good enough shape to talk sense into her mother that she almost believed it too. Connie hoped it would be possible. She was far too practical to fall into the trap of hope, taking a more 'I'll believe it when I see it' approach to life.

When had she become so callous? When Mitchel had been taken by the freak boating accident? For a whole lot of years after, she'd wished it had been her and not her baby brother who'd died. They'd been thick as thieves, calling themselves the Two Musketeers. Being the older sister, she'd always taken on responsibility for him. If Mitchel had a question on his homework, he came to her; if he wanted to sneak an extra snack from the kitchen, she negotiated with the kitchen staff; if he wanted to go to the movies, she made the arrangements while their mother tended to the senator and his career. Her mother had loved them, though. Connie could see it in her mother's eyes and in the warm hugs she'd give before heading out to some fundraiser or charity dinner. Her mother would often times be dressed in a beautiful sparkly evening dress, looking more like a princess to Connie than a politician's wife. Her mother's makeup would be impeccable and her hair in some sweeping updo that Connie would practice on her own hair in the mirror long past bedtime while Mitchel built a fort. Before her mother would finally acquiesce to an impatient husband's demand that she *get a move on*, she would whisper into Connie's ear, *Take care of each other.*

A surprising tear rolled down her cheek at the memory. She turned toward the passenger window to hide her face from Barrett, and wiped the rogue tear.

"I asked her once if she would ever leave him," she recalled the moment so clearly. They were in the restroom of this fancy downtown hotel for a fundraiser. Her mother had just knocked back a second glass of wine while pretending to apply a fresh coat of lipstick. Connie had joined her mother when her stepfather started fidgeting in his seat, looking around. He wasn't pleased that her mother was taking so long to get back from the bathroom. He was antsy, so Connie did what she always did and excused herself from the table to go check on her mother. There'd been too many times she'd found her slumped against the bathroom stall passed out. And even though that hadn't happened in years, the memories had imprinted into Connie's brain. She became hardwired to worry about her mother if she took too long getting to the car or going to the bathroom, especially at a function like a fundraiser. Most of the time, she was able to pull herself together but not always.

Connie had hated seeing her mother so dependent on a man, and she'd sworn at a young age never to put herself in the same situation.

"What did she say?" he asked, clearing his throat first, and she realized she'd zoned out for a few seconds.

"That marriage was forever and she couldn't just walk away. She asked where she would go anyway in this defeated tone that used to make me so mad. She had a point, though. Everything in her life was wrapped up around the senator and his life. Her friends were other politician's wives who'd signed up for the long haul too," she explained, and on some level, the reasoning had made sense. No one should go into a marriage with the thought it was a test run and that they'd 'see' if it worked out.

Having a front row view of a manipulative and emotionally abusive marriage, Connie had sworn off the institution from a young age. Why do it at all, had been her thinking. Being grown now, Connie's perspective on divorce had shifted. There was absolutely no reason to stay in any relationship that no longer worked, especially when one of the partners was manipulative and abusive. Granted, it was best if the tendencies were discovered early on before the relationship could evolve into a forever pact. But master manipulators didn't show their cards right away. Their actions were like a frog in a pot of water. Turn the heat up one degree at a time and the frog never bothered to jump out. It never even realized what was happening until it was too late, if even then.

"I believe in the institution for other people,"

Barrett said after a thoughtful pause. "Never much thought it was a good idea for myself."

"Did your parents have a bad marriage?" she asked.

"I couldn't tell you one way or the other," he stated. "I have no real memories of them together. If I did and they were bad, I most likely suppressed them."

"That would be a nice ability to have," she said. "I'm sorry that you never got to know your mother, though."

"It means a lot to hear you say that," he said with a warmth in his voice that lit half a dozen campfires inside her. "More than you realize."

She reached over and squeezed his forearm. The familiar jolt of electricity from contact comforted her now rather than caught her off guard.

"Do you mind checking the news again?" Barrett asked. He had a habit of changing the subject when they got on the topic of his background. She could only imagine the devastation of losing a mother while being so young and how that would shape him. It was clear the two of them had the same views on marriage. Neither wanted nor craved taking part in that institution.

Now? Being around Barrett caused her to re-examine her old views. Strange how her stance had never made her feel like she was missing out on something before meeting Barrett.

CHAPTER ELEVEN

The sky was overcast, threatening to storm without the droplets. It made for good driving conditions. Barrett figured they'd be in Austin by dinner time at this pace. He would prefer to roll into his city after dark to provide a little extra protection from other people's eyes. Seeing inside a vehicle was much more difficult at night.

A half dozen thoughts rolled around in his mind, each fighting for center stage. Could he reach out to one of his brothers for a new ride? Would their communications be compromised? The likelihood of Dirty Joe being able to hack into their cell communications with all the encryption was low. However, the decision to put his brothers' lives potentially at risk wasn't something Barrett would take lightly, even though they were all grown men capable of taking care of themselves. All of his brothers were law enforcement trained and active in their professions. Harding was still healing from a gunshot wound that Barrett could now relate to. He was grateful his shoulder wasn't in worse shape. Under normal circumstances, he might have dropped by the ER. Now, it was too late for stitches; there would be a scar, and that was it as long as he could keep the wound from infection.

They had enough supplies to handle his shoulder and Connie's gash. Together, they were quite the pair. He almost laughed out loud. Laughing had a way of breaking up tension. He'd learned the lesson a long time ago on the job. While an outsider might be offended by him and his fellow Marshals if they heard them joking around during tense times, Barrett knew that it was a release valve. No one took each other too seriously.

More unwanted thoughts shoved their way to center stage. The comment Connie had made about never wanting to get married made a whole lot of sense to him after hearing about her mom and stepdad. Marriage must have seemed like a prison sentence to her while growing up. Her position on the institution mirrored his, so it struck him as odd that he wished more for her.

The thought of a life alone, his life alone, was a sudden gut punch and came out of thin air.

It wasn't his business what Connie decided to do with the rest of her life. He had enough on his plate dealing with his own feelings about matrimony—feelings that were starting to shift as he got closer to his fortieth birthday. What was it about those birthday years that ended in zero that had him reevaluating his life choices?

"I overheard my mother whispering to or about Thorogood Hammond," Connie said low and under her breath.

"Isn't he a land developer?" he asked.

"I believe so," she said. "He runs a successful company." She shook her head. "He's probably just a campaign contributor."

Barrett kept his gaze on the stretch of road in front of them. Millionaires and politicians. Two types of folks he preferred to avoid at all costs.

"I got something that I think you need to know about," Connie said, her tone came off as a warning that made him sit up a little straighter in his seat. "I'll just read the report."

Barrett tightened his grip on the steering wheel until his knuckles turned white.

"An officer has been barricaded into an apartment building and all communication has been cut off. A service weapon, badge, and Kevlar vest was tossed out the second-story window of the downtown apartment building two blocks from the University of Texas campus minutes after the officer stopped responding to calls on the radio. This is believed to be a developing hostage situation. The chief of police is not giving additional details at this time. Chief Rogan did say, however, that he will hold a press conference at five p.m." Connie sat quietly for a few beats. "One of your brothers works for Austin PD."

The statement landed a sucker punch to his solar plexus, which was how he knew Crawford had to be the officer in question. It was almost like a sixth sense kicked in under these circumstances, causing the words to resonate if they were true.

"Yes," was all he said as the wheels in his brain churned in hyperdrive. "His name is Crawford."

"I'm so sorry, Barrett," she said thickly, like she was on the verge of tears. "This is terrible, and it's my fault that you're here and not there."

"Don't do that," he said to her, as he realized she also blamed herself for her brother's death. "I was heading toward the cabin no matter what. I just happened to find you along the way and, for both of our sakes, I couldn't be more thankful that I found you when I did. Me leaving Austin had nothing to do with you and everything to do with my decisions. You're not responsible for other people's actions, Connie."

She didn't immediately respond as she turned toward the passenger window again. He noticed she'd done it before when she cried.

"My brother is a capable law enforcement officer," Barrett reassured, hoping Dirty Joe wasn't responsible. Plus, other than a gut feeling, he didn't have proof it was Crawford in that apartment being held against his will. There were just shy of two thousand officers on the force. The odds were in Crawford's favor.

Until Barrett considered the situation as it stood. Throwing a weapon out the window made some sense to Barrett, but why the badge? The vest made no sense to toss either, because the perp could have put it on himself. And why a second-story apartment where cops could surround the building? The moves were bold and flashy. They were calculated to draw the most attention to shove it in Barrett's face. Show him who was boss and redeem a fallen leader to his underlings.

"I need to reach out to my family members," Barrett finally said. "See where they are and what they know."

"Do you want me to call and put them on speaker?" Connie asked.

"I'd rather pull over and talk to them without the distraction of driving," he stated. "Saw a sign for a rest stop that should be coming up here in the next few minutes. I can hold off until then."

"Since this is a standoff with the police, the senator will muscle his way in," Connie said.

"Good," Barrett said. His comment seemed to catch her off guard. "Then, we'll know where he is, and it'll make it easier to find him."

The comment perked her up.

"I'll see my mom too," she said. "She's always required to accompany him when there is big news, and he'll be there to support the mayor who will, in turn, be there to support the police chief."

"As messed up and unthinkable as this situation is, it's also quite possibly the break we need," he said to Connie, wishing like everything that it didn't have to involve his younger brother. But Barrett also knew his brother well enough to realize Crawford always kept a small backup weapon strapped to his ankle. Whoever was holding him against his will—and he could only assume he was right about this being Crawford at this point—wouldn't realize Crawford had a secondary weapon. It was the first spark of hope in this whole scenario.

"It's difficult to see anything positive right now," she said.

"Agreed," he responded. "Without hope, there is nothing left to fight for."

"Hope is something I gave up on a long time ago,"

she admitted. "But in your brother's case, I'd bust down any wall to find it and hold onto it again."

Those words were balm to a broken soul. He couldn't help but wonder if his stance on marriage would be different if he'd met someone like Connie years ago. Then again, there was no doubt in his mind that she was one of a kind. His heart wondered if he would have had the brains to realize how special she was all those years ago.

A little voice in the back of his mind said there was a reason she'd come into his life at this point. She was special and he was finally mature enough to see it.

Right now though, those thoughts needed to be shelved.

A sign indicated the rest stop was on the next exit, so he veered off the highway and pulled into the rest area. A few cars were parked three to four spaces away from each other, giving plenty of room for privacy. Barrett took the very first spot, making it easy to turn his back on the other drivers and passengers. Being seen still might put him at risk if the situation in Austin didn't pan out, and if whoever was after Connie remained at large. The senator had clearly hired professionals to do the job for him, as Barrett would expect. No doubt people were used that would make it near impossible to trace back to the politician. Discrediting Connie was different from killing her; Barrett had taken note of the distinction before, and the thought kept circling back.

Did it mean the senator had a soft spot for his adopted daughter? Barrett filed the information away, noting it might come in handy later on as he cut off the engine of the Chevy.

"I'll be right back," Connie said, motioning toward the restrooms.

He nodded, repositioning in his seat so he could keep one eye trained on the door to the ladies' room. "Keep your head down when you walk, okay?"

"Got it," she said with a smile, seeming to appreciate the reminder and show of concern.

She exited as he made the call to Harding and held the phone to his ear. As unlikely as it was that someone in this rest stop had the ability or resources to enable them to hear the call, Barrett had learned a long time ago to leave nothing to chance. So, he opted for a regular call instead of putting Harding on speaker.

But first, he sent a text to let his brother know the unknown, untraceable number that was about to show up on his phone as a call was actually Barrett. They had a number code 07734 that, when turned upside down, loosely spelled the word *hello*.

Harding picked up on the first ring.

"Where are you?" he immediately asked, then added, "never mind. Don't answer that."

"I'm safe for now," Barrett said, and that was about as much as he could promise. Anything more and they both knew he'd be reaching for good news that wasn't there. "Is it Crawford?"

"Everyone has tried to reach him," Harding said on a sharp sigh. "He would have responded to one of us if he could have."

Barrett muttered a string of curses under his breath. "What do you know about the situation so far?" he asked. With his family working in law enforcement, he hoped they would be privileged to more information than the media. Lawson, the youngest, was a K-9 officer at Austin PD.

"The same as you," Harding admitted. "Lawson said he can't talk about what's going on until he gets approval from his SO."

"Sounds about right, but I was hoping for more," Barrett said, watching as Connie disappeared into the building. His pulse kicked up a few notches at losing visual contact with her for more reasons than just his growing attraction to her.

"We all were, bro. But, man, I'm so relieved to hear from you after that last text," Harding said. His relief was evident in his tone.

"Sorry that I had to go about it that way, but—"

"No need to apologize. We all have the plan," Harding quickly countered. "I knew you wouldn't enact it without carefully considering your options."

"I was on my way back when I found out the news," Barrett said. "Turns out, I'm no good at running. Not even when it's probably the smartest thing to do."

"Some plans sound better on paper than they turn out to be in practice," Harding agreed. "I understand why you did what you did."

Those words provided more comfort than Harding could possibly realize.

"Exactly," Barrett said. "But here we are, with Crawford being held hostage, and I think we both know it's because of me."

"You did your job," Harding pointed out.

"I know," Barrett said but appreciated his brother

saying so nonetheless. "And we both know the hazards and are willing to take the risks. It's just hard when the consequences come down on your family member and not directly on you."

"We won't let the bastard win this one." Harding's confidence put a little more of the wind back in Barrett's sails. "Dirty Joe is going down, just like he did before. And this time, the state is going to have to follow through on their end of the bargain and keep him locked up. He should never be allowed out of solitary confinement considering his disrespect for law enforcement officials who are doing their jobs."

When his brother put it like that, some of the weight that had been bearing down on Barrett's shoulders since hearing the news about Crawford lifted. Barrett wouldn't rest until his brother was safe and Dirty Joe was back in handcuffs where he belonged. It was going to be okay. He would make sure of it.

"The AG had better make certain of it," Barrett said, referring to the Attorney General.

"The governor is involved, as well as several senators. This story is blowing up and the state won't be able to afford to let Dirty Joe loose again," Harding pointed out. "Not on their watches. Plus, there's already a huge backlash brewing over the man escaping Huntsville in the first place. The warden will lose his job over this. Things will change. They'll have to."

The media could be a useful tool in bringing awareness to people who would make sure change happened. Some of his tension eased.

Barrett wouldn't be able to sigh relief until he got a visual on Connie. She'd been gone longer than he wanted her to be, and his pulse kicked up a couple of notches with each passing minute. When the door opened and she appeared, a tsunami of relief slammed into him.

"I need a vehicle," he said to his brother.

"At the same place we talked about?" Harding immediately caught on.

"That's right," Barrett confirmed as Connie slipped in the Chevy and claimed her seat.

"It'll be there long before you arrive," Harding reassured. "Anything else? Cash? Clothes?"

"Got all of those already," Barrett said.

"I figured as much," Harding said.

"Any chance you can meet?" Barrett didn't want to go into the details of having Connie with him on the call.

"I'll be inside," Harding said. "ETA?"

"A couple of hours tops," he said. If their assumptions were correct, and Dirty Joe was holding Crawford hostage to draw Barrett out, giving out a little bit of vague information like this on the call wasn't completely out of line. He hoped.

"See you then, bro," Harding confirmed.

Barrett brought his right index finger up to his lips as an indicator for Connie to remain silent as he ended the call with Harding.

"How did it go?" she asked, not seeming to be fazed by the request.

"Good," Barrett said as he started the Chevy. "I'll fill you in on the way."

Connie reclaimed her seat and buckled in. No

amount of shoulder pain could stop him from leaning over the bench seat to kiss her.

His injury screamed at him, but he couldn't regret the choice. Besides, their current plan had them driving straight into the fire.

CHAPTER TWELVE

Connie leaned into the kiss, careful not to inflict pain on Barrett's injury. The second their lips had touched, the overwhelming feeling of being home filled her. It was a place she'd never known before Barrett. She'd never known to expect this much out of a...*relationship*, or whatever this thing happening between them could be categorized as.

Or maybe it was too early to define it at all. Maybe it was best to let it be what it was.

There were no guarantees that either or both were going to make it out alive. So, maybe they should just enjoy this moment and let tomorrow do its thing. Take them wherever it wanted them to go.

If they were alive tomorrow.

She couldn't think about those things while his lips were melted into hers, and she breathed in his woodsy and masculine scent. He was being in the woods after a spring rain, and she was finally becoming an outdoor person.

Barrett pulled back, then said, "I've been wanting to do that all morning."

"Next time, don't wait," she said, more than a little breathless. He had that effect on her and she smiled because he was breathing heavily too. Their sexual chemistry was like nothing she'd ever experienced, and she could only imagine what making love would be like.

For now, she tabled the thought. Her brain wanted to think about anything besides the task ahead. As much as Connie wanted to see her mother and know she was safe, she dreaded the possibility of coming face-to-face with her stepfather. And she had yet to figure out how she was going to take him down with the evidence she had against him. As much as she couldn't stand the man, she hated the idea of hurting another human being. In some ways, it made her feel like she was stooping to his level when she really wanted to find high ground. Too late for a family reunion considering the man was trying to destroy her. And what would her mother be left with? A son who died tragically and a daughter who was murdered by someone who was supposed to protect her.

One way or the other, it was going to be over soon enough.

"Harding is going to meet us when we get to Austin." Barrett's voice broke into her thoughts. "He'll have a vehicle for us, so we can safely make the switch. And backup if needed. I'd like the two of us to stick together, which presents risks for you that you should think through before deciding. Being with me could cause you to be seen before you're ready."

"The same goes for you," she pointed out.

"Yes," he said. "The other thing I should mention is that my brother doesn't know about you. There wasn't time to get into it on the phone, and I thought it might be best if the two of you meet in person, instead of having to explain your situation while we're on the road."

"I figured when I opened the door that was the case," she said. "It's a good plan and I would have said the same thing if I'd been here."

He nodded.

It was interesting to note how much they seemed to think alike. She was molded by a lifetime spent growing up in the same house as her stepfather. He'd taught her to suspect first and always be on alert. Trust no one. Folks who worked in law enforcement were trained to do the same. Nature of the beast, she guessed.

"Do we have a plan other than to meet up with your brother?" she asked.

"Harding and the rest of my family will be watching the hostage situation develop. They'll likely have a plan of attack or at the very least the beginnings of one," he said. "We'll have to inform them of your situation, so they can factor that into the equation. We're pretty much experts at pivoting when necessary. And we're all used to complications cropping up from seemingly out of the blue considering we all work in the same field."

He shot her a look, when he seemed to catch onto the fact he'd just called her a complication.

"I didn't mean that in a bad way," he quickly backtracked.

She reached out and placed her hand on his forearm. "I know. I didn't take it wrong."

Barrett exhaled as though he'd been holding the breath longer than he should.

"What you said about not being able to stand hiding out," she began. "Well, I couldn't agree more. As much as I didn't want to leave the cabin for reasons that had nothing to do with facing down my stepfather, I wouldn't want to hide like I'd done something wrong. After getting a good night of sleep and my bearings, I was ready to face this and put it behind me. And no matter how this ends—"

"Don't do that," he said to her. "Don't even make it possible in your mind this could go south. Going into this with one hundred percent confidence that justice will land on top is the best mindset."

"I think I read about Navy SEALs who do the same thing," she said. "Or maybe it was on Netflix. All I can remember is how one of them said before a mission, he takes ten minutes to visualize what he's going to be doing later that day. He said he goes into detail because it makes him focus more."

"Mindset is everything when going into battle," he agreed.

"It's the reason you smile, isn't it?" she asked. "You always get this grin on your face whenever we've been faced with serious danger or talk about what we might be facing when it's serious."

"I didn't realize I still did that, to be honest," he said with a chuckle. "But, yes, it's a way of sticking up a middle finger to anything that threatens to take my life."

"Facing fear is probably your specialty then," she said, admiring his ability. "Wish I could say the same."

"You're doing just fine," he countered. "You have an unbelievable dignity and strength that most folks could only wish for. Don't be so hard on yourself, because I'd ride beside you as my partner any day of the week."

A rogue thought that she wished the offer extended to life, and not just for work, shot through her mind. She dismissed it as quickly as if she'd just touched a hot stove. There was no room in the Chevy for thoughts of that nature.

"Your confidence in me is much appreciated," she said honestly as traffic thickened, a sure sign they were getting closer to Austin.

The rest of the ride was spent in companionable silence, each lost in their own thoughts.

Connie's kept circling back to wishing something permanent could come out of her relationship with Barrett. She chalked it up to facing death. It was probably just biology wanting her to latch onto life with both hands.

Or could she actually be falling in love with Barrett Quinn?

———

Barrett pulled into the parking lot of Hotel Rain, a five-star hotel near Congress Avenue with a view of the river along with the bat bridge. Here, folks could pay extra for a balcony facing the bridge, where they could sit out at sunset in the summer and watch hundreds of bats emerge all at once. It was quite a sight and folks came from all over the state for the privilege of watching. In

November, however, there was no such spectacle to behold, which also meant slightly less foot traffic areas they drove past.

The reason Barrett and Harding had settled on this hotel was for the ability to hand over keys to a valet and have a vehicle hidden within minutes. The manager had a relationship with their uncle—for reasons Barrett didn't want to know—but it netted preferential treatment for them, and an escape when necessary. Hotel Rain was a safe haven.

Barrett pulled the Chevy right up to the valet, who looked at it with a smile. These guys were trained to treat every customer like a rockstar no matter what they drove or wore. Plenty of wealthy cattle ranchers showed up here driving a dirty pickup truck and wearing jeans and boots.

"This place is gorgeous," Connie said with awe. "I've driven by, but I've never been inside."

He brought her up to speed on the situation a second before the valet opened her door.

"Ma'am," the brown-haired, brown-eyed twenty-something year old said.

She thanked him as she exited the Chevy. He jogged around to the driver's side and did the same for Barrett.

"Mind keeping her out of the rain?" Barrett asked, knowing it would mean the valet would have to park her in the garage and out of street view.

"Not a problem, sir," Brown Eyes said with a smile. He slipped into the driver's seat and disappeared a few seconds later.

Barrett reached for Connie's hand and then clasped

their fingers together. There was something about holding her hand that made the world right itself. The hotel lobby was expansive; high ceilings, crystal chandeliers, basically the works. No expense was spared building this hotel, and its room prices reflected the investment. The cheapest room started at eight hundred dollars a night. Barrett didn't care how many zeroes he had in his bank account, there weren't many occasions he could bring himself to spend money unnecessarily on something like a hotel room.

But right now, his thoughts were on Crawford and he prayed Harding had an update. The bar was tucked around the backside of the elevator bank and there were plenty of secluded tables and little alcoves. It was the second thing he and his brother liked about the place. This was the spot to meet if privacy was imperative.

"We might have to walk around a little bit before we find him," he began, when a hand on his left shoulder caught him off guard. He spun around and came face-to-face with his best friend and brother.

Harding brought Barrett into a bear hug, and he couldn't regret the mind-numbing shoulder pain that came with movement. The two embraced for a good long time and it was beyond great to be standing here with his brother. Again, it struck him how horrible it would have been to lose one of his brothers—and worse yet if he'd only had one—when they were kids. They'd done a whole bunch of stupid things while out on the cattle ranch that could have easily gone wrong. There'd been a few broken bones and close encounters with wild boar and other dangerous wildlife, but they'd all come out the other end of childhood intact.

His heart broke again for Connie and her loss. He wished there was something he could do to make it better, knowing full well he would never be able to soothe her pain.

Right now, though, he could relate to her as he faced the absolute horror of Crawford's situation. Since time was of the essence, he pulled back from the hug and introduced Harding to Connie.

"It's a pleasure to meet you," Harding said to her, and she practically beamed back at him. Seeing the two of them together stirred something in Barrett's heart that he didn't have time to dissect, but knew from the depths of his soul he needed to at some point in the near future. Harding's gaze lingered on her injured forehead, but he seemed to think better of asking about it right now.

"Same here," she said to him, and then the two surprised him with giving each other a brief hug. Since that wasn't something Harding normally did with someone who wasn't family, Barrett nearly lost it in a good way.

"How about we get out of the main bar area and take a booth over here," Harding said, directing them to their favorite one by a small waterfall. The noise would also muffle their conversation even more from prying ears.

They followed him after Barrett placed his hand on the small of Connie's back and then sat at the round table before hunkering over to speak in quiet conversations.

"Do I want to know what happened to your shoulder?" Harding immediately asked.

"A story for another time," Barrett reassured. "Once we put all this behind us and Crawford is safe."

"Speaking of our brother, Lawson confirmed it is Crawford being held hostage, and the police chief is trying to limit the information that gets out in the media. They've evacuated the small apartment complex and have set up a perimeter," Harding stated.

"Any demands?" Barrett asked on the off chance this wasn't related to his predicament.

Harding shook his head.

"Strange, isn't it?" Connie asked. "Wouldn't the person have something to say?"

"He doesn't want to reveal his identity yet," Barrett said.

"That would be my guess too," Harding confirmed. "This way, no one is certain and it makes profiling a whole lot more difficult."

"He knows I'll come for Crawford," Barrett said. "I'd gladly trade places with my brother. It's me that he wants anyway. Our brother is innocent."

"All we know so far is what I already told you, and that Crawford wasn't on a call when he was taken hostage. There's speculation there's a little boy and girl being held as well, but this is yet to be confirmed. Two kids *have* gone missing in the area according to their babysitter; the mom is a single parent and was at work when her babysitter called to say the kids had been taken from the playground. She'd been distracted for a few minutes by someone asking for directions," Harding informed.

"Which could mean more than one person is involved. One guy keeps the babysitter occupied while another snatches them practically underneath her nose," Barrett said as Connie involuntarily shivered. It was probably difficult for a civilian to hear the two of them talk about something horrific, like it was as an everyday event and as uneventful as going to the grocery.

Barrett had a whole lot of experience separating out his emotions when it came to a case. The worse the case, the easier it became to hit the shutoff valve. All it took was for him to remind himself that the less personal he made the crime, the more he could focus. When he was able to focus without distractions, the probability of a successful ending flew through the roof.

So, yes, he *could* push aside his anger and indignation in order to lock up the perp and save kids and families from getting news they'd never be able to recover from, like death.

"There is a father involved and he's threatened to take the children in the past. No one can reach him, so it's possible the timing is a coincidence and the kids are with him," Harding explained.

"Anything's possible," Barrett stated, knowing they had to consider every angle, but that the obvious one was usually correct. The irony of the siblings being brother and sister was not lost on him given his current company.

Connie was taking the news about as well as could be expected under the circumstances. Her chin might be up but her eyes told the real story, and he loved her even more for her compassion.

Loved?

Barrett shoved the word aside and moved on, even though his heart wanted to put up an argument to stay put.

CHAPTER THIRTEEN

"What's our best move?" Barrett asked his brother as Connie tried to figure out how she played into all this. "How do we convince the police chief to let me negotiate a trade?"

"No," Connie said, leaving no room for doubt that she disapproved of the idea. There was no way she could stand by and allow that to happen. Panic tightened her chest, making it next to impossible to breathe. "He'll kill you immediately. You won't even make it through the front door. The minute he sees you, it's game over."

"She's right," Harding said quietly. "We both know it. You'd be playing right into his hands."

Barrett sat there for a long moment before finally conceding with a slight nod. "Then, what? Because I thought about it on the ride over, and I can't think of one idea to get Crawford out of this and Dirty Joe back in handcuffs without blood being spilled."

"Plus, there's a complication," Connie said to a

confused-looking Harding, unwilling and unable to let him continue down that path for a second longer.

"And that is?" he asked.

"Me." She meant that word on more than one level and hoped the connection they shared would be enough for him to consider coming up with a different plan. She couldn't bring herself to make eye contact when she was feeling so vulnerable. She slowly exhaled the moment his hand covered hers and gave a reassuring squeeze and then explained her situation with her stepfather and whoever he'd hired to do his bidding.

"Right. We do have to factor in Senator Owens and the men he seems to have employed," Harding agreed when no one else spoke.

"Not just that," Barrett added before letting go of her hand. She missed the warmth of skin-to-skin contact immediately. "We need a plan to get to Connie's mother." He went on to explain the e-mail.

"Can we authenticate the e-mail? Make sure it actually came from her mother?" Harding asked.

"There's no way to know if she wrote it or not. My stepfather would have access to her e-mail. He could have written it. Without being able to contact my mother or get a message to her, there's no way to be certain," she said, hating the helpless feeling that was trying to take hold. There was no way she would let him win and drag her mother to the pits along with him. Not this time. Not as long as Connie had air in her lungs. Not as long as she still had a voice.

"We have enough hands on deck to get a message to your mother," Harding said to Connie. "The only thing we don't have is a whole lot of time."

"The press conference," Connie said. "My mother will be there to support her husband. Could we split up and possibly contact her that way?"

"I don't like the idea of you being anywhere near the site," Barrett stated, and his protectiveness warmed her heart. Truth be known, she felt the same way about him going anywhere near that apartment. But they were not in an ideal situation, so chances had to be taken.

"I don't have to be the one to slip my mother a note, but she has to be able to see me," she pointed out. "Otherwise, she won't trust it."

Barrett's nod seemed reluctant. He had to realize her mother would be suspicious of anything that didn't come directly from Connie. Plus, they were taking a huge risk in trusting her mother in the first place. As much as Connie didn't want to believe her mother could be brainwashed, the senator could be very convincing and her mother hadn't been in her right mind in years. He'd continued to wear her down over time. And yet, those recent sparks of life in her mother's eyes weren't figments of Connie's imagination. Everyone had a tipping point. Had her mother finally reached hers? Was she ready to pick up her life and move on?

"Naomi wants to help. No one knows who she is, and she can possibly get close enough to slip a note to your mother," Harding said. A woman might slip past security easier than a man.

"That would be amazing," Connie responded, figuring it might just work. "Except that I don't want to put anyone in unnecessary danger. The senator won't care who she is if she steps on his toes or threatens his image in any way."

"My fiancée is aware of the risk," Harding stated.

"How will Naomi get past security?" Connie asked. "There will be a lot and quite a few of them will be in plain clothes."

"Lawson works the K-9 unit for Austin PD," Harding explained. "He can slip her past any blockades. From there, she might be on her own."

"The focus will be on the senator, so that could work," Connie reasoned. It was still a whole lot of risk, and there were no guarantees Naomi would be able to get within ten feet of Connie's mother. Making a scene would only put undo attention on Harding's fiancée and that could be deadly. "Still, it's my family. He's after me and so I should be the one to face him. I *want* to be the one to do it." She turned to Barrett, knowing full well he would object the loudest. "It's like you said before. You'd rather face your enemy and take your chances than die with a knife in your back from running."

"That's not exactly what I said," Barrett jumped in. His face twisted in a mix of distress and worry. His mouth opened to speak and she was certain he was ready to put up an argument as to why the same rule didn't apply to her. Instead, he exhaled and his chest deflated. "As much as I don't like it, you do bring up a good point. It's not fair for me to say I have to be the one to step in to save Crawford, while trying to talk you out of standing up for your mother."

Harding had picked up a napkin and was tearing little pieces off the edges as a waitress appeared seemingly out of nowhere.

"Would anyone like to place a drink order?" she asked, paying particular attention to the men at the table. She was dressed in a tuxedo and had her long brunette hair slicked off her face and pulled into a low ponytail.

It probably shouldn't rankle Connie that the wait-ress didn't seem to realize there was another person at the table. She'd most likely been trained on how to make the most tips. Paying attention to the ones she figured would pay the bill seemed like an outdated prac-tice, but it wasn't an unusual tactic.

Barrett and Harding deferred to Connie in unison.

"Coffee would be nice," she said, thinking it was getting chilly outside and they would most likely be leaving soon.

"Same for me," Harding said, as Barrett ordered the same.

"Three coffees coming right up," Brunette hid her disappointment. Her gaze locked onto Connie for a few seconds longer than was comfortable. As much as Connie didn't want to be paranoid, she also realized how far her stepfather's reach was in this town. Did he frequent this place too?

Nothing surprised her.

"Any sugar or creamer?" the waitress asked.

"None for me," Connie responded, knowing full well the question was meant for her. Didn't women drink black coffee in her world?

The men also shook their heads.

"All right then," she said. "I'll be right back." With that, she placed coasters on the table and then disappeared.

"We can try to come up with a workable plan, but at the end of the day, I think my situation is going to come down to a lot of luck," Connie stated. "I would, however, like to pass along the location of the evidence that I have against him to one of you guys for safe-keeping."

"That's it," Barrett said, sitting up a little straighter in his seat. "You need to get a message to him that if anything happens to you, we're instructed to release the recording to the media. Threaten him with the AG. Let him know law enforcement officials are holding onto the..."

"Drive," she stated. "I put the recording on a thumb drive before destroying my cell so he couldn't track me."

"Okay," Barrett continued with a nod of approval, "the drive and say they have no idea what they're hanging onto. If news breaks that anything has happened to you, it's over for him."

Connie thought about the idea for a long moment. Something popped.

"Your cell is encrypted, right?" she asked Barrett.

"Yes." He confirmed what she already knew as the waitress came back with a tray on the flat of her palm. Conversation stalled as Barrett handed over his cell and the waitress passed out their coffees.

"Thank you," Harding said to her, essentially dismissing her with a nod.

"I know the senator's cell number by heart. All I have to do is make the threat and let him know that I mean business," Connie said, taking the phone being offered to her. "Do you mind? Letting him know will provide insurance that I won't be shot on sight."

"Go for it," Barrett said. "I've been needing to test the security of the phone anyway."

"Here goes nothing." Connie took in a sharp breath and then crafted the message. She closed by saying he could absolutely believe this was the real her and offered proof in the form of telling him something only she would know. The code to the fake door that led to a panic room from his closet.

Those three little dots indicating a response was being crafted appeared immediately. Connie's heart sank to her toes. She held her breath, waiting, her gaze unable to stray from the screen.

Come home ASAP. It's not what you think. I'm the target.

Those last three words made her want to embrace hope. "Is that even possible?"

"Ask him who is behind the threat then," Barrett stated, folding his arms across his chest. This information seemed to catch him off guard too. She could almost see the wheels turning in his mind.

She sent the response.

???

Will talk when you get home.

"Granted, he might not want to give a name via a text message, when he couldn't be one hundred percent certain I'm not being tortured into this," she reasoned. "If he honestly doesn't know who is behind this and we can take it on faith that he isn't behind my kidnapping —which is a big leap at this point—do I dare risk trusting him? I overheard him essentially ordering a hit *on me*. I recorded the back half of the conversation. Not admissible in court, I know, but the mass public will convict him when they hear his voice and his political career will be over."

———

This new information would change things for Connie, if not for Barrett.

"I'm inclined to believe him," Barrett said. His instincts were generally spot-on, and he was heavily relying on them now. "Someone trying to blackmail him could want to use you and not kill you. The person who drugged you could have murdered you right then and there. You were knocked out for a little while and have no memories of what happened."

"I don't know what to believe," Harding admitted as his eyebrow shot up. His gaze had lingered on her forehead but to his credit he hadn't taken time to ask questions. He must have had them. "But if you give the location of the evidence to me, I'll make certain it stays safe until you can sort it out and find the truth. If the senator is guilty, we'll make sure the man faces justice."

"I guess there's no harm in seeing if he's being honest," she stated. "If he wants me dead, he'll have his chance but not without his career going down the drain."

"It wouldn't make any sense," Barrett started, "unless he thinks you're bluffing about giving the evidence to a law enforcement official."

Barrett wanted to say that tracking down dangerous felons, handcuffing them, and turning them in, didn't always mean they would stay off the streets. His current dilemma proved that justice wasn't always served.

"He should know me better than that by now," she said. "I don't bluff, and I think he would call it if he thought I was. He didn't try to convince me that what I had was wrong. He essentially said he was being framed."

Was she being too hopeful? Was he? Because he hated to see a family that could never mend fences. But the damage in this one might be irreparable. Barrett hoped not, for Connie's sake *and* her mother's. Besides, it was unfathomable to Barrett that a family member would put a hit out on her. And yet, based on everything she'd shared with Barrett about her stepfather so far, the man wasn't exactly a saint. He was a class-A jerk when it came to being a father. Even with that knowledge, Barrett leaned toward trusting the man in this case. The evidence pointed to someone else being involved, considering someone had to be on the other end of the conversation she'd recorded who also seemed to want her dead.

"Your stepfather would be a target to many and, most likely, have a long list of enemies," Barrett reasoned. Politicians had to play their cards just right or risk revenge. If he took money from someone but didn't deliver on a promise he made, he could easily get on someone's bad side. Politics and power were potent bedfellows. Cross the wrong person and it could mean lights out forever.

"Why come after me, though?" she asked. It was a good question.

"Someone drugged you, put makeup on you, and dressed you in clothes that you said didn't belong to you," Barrett recalled. "They might not have been trying to kill you after all. It's possible the person was trying to discredit you by taking compromising photos. We already discussed the possibility before, even when we believed your stepfather could be the one behind the acts. You got away and the person might not have felt they could risk you remembering who they were or being able to testify against them." Barrett paused. "What if the person was trying to blackmail your stepfather into doing something by compromising you?"

"If there's any truth about the senator, it would be that image is everything to him," she said. "He could lose his bid for presidency if something terrible surfaced about his only daughter."

"Hunter Owens is seriously planning a run for the Oval Office?" Harding asked, not hiding the shock in his voice.

"Yes, but the news isn't widely known outside of political circles," she admitted.

"I heard there was talk, but nothing had been confirmed and you know how these rumors go. That alone could cause someone to target you," Harding said. "Especially if there were compromising photos involved. The senator sounds like the kind of person who would go to great lengths to cover up the possibility of bad press."

"He is," she agreed.

"Does he have someone running against him who poses a direct threat, or is less than honest?" Harding asked.

Connie shot a look that said Harding couldn't possibly be that naïve. Politics and backstabbing? Politics and murder? Yes and yes.

"I'm on the right side of the law, very clear about my mission," Harding said by way of defense. Then cracked a small smile. "My career choice looks better every day.

I know exactly who my enemy is and how I'll plan to go about finding him. Politics sounds like layers of lies and deception."

"There are folks in it for the right reasons," she said. "I've known people who were worth admiring. They wanted to make the state a better place for everyone and not just those lining their pockets."

"Those are the ones we like to have in office," Harding said. "They have our backs when we need them to, which is very important in our line of work."

"Speaking of having someone's back," Barrett said. "Any news on Crawford while we finish coming up with a plan for Connie?"

"Nothing so far," Harding said on a shrug. The notion their brother might already be dead was written in the concern lines on Harding's face. Crawford was a standup officer. One of the best Austin PD had to offer. Still, him being locked up with a man who had already murdered two U.S. Marshals wasn't exactly reassuring.

"Dirty Joe is waiting it out," Barrett said. "He knows I'll come." And the man was right. The only question was how to do it without giving him a reason to kill Crawford right in front of Barrett's face. This was revenge and Dirty Joe would go to any length to make Barrett suffer.

"I agree that sitting here and doing nothing isn't the play," Harding agreed. "It would be nice if one good idea would take shape."

"The area will be crowded," Barrett warned, wondering if there was a way to accomplish their task without unnecessarily putting innocent citizens at risk.

"I say we go in for both targets at the same time,"

Connie said. "The best way to find out if my stepfather is being honest is through my mother. Being in a public place might make it harder to pull off murdering me. The person could end up getting cold feet. If that's what we're dealing with."

"There will be a lot of law enforcement there if the governor is part of the press conference," Barrett reasoned. "They'll check the rooftops for shooters."

"Does that mean we're going?" Connie asked. The renewed hope in her voice said that she prayed her stepfather wasn't that ruthless.

"Looks like it," Barrett confirmed with a look toward Harding.

His brother nodded. They were going all-in and with very little in the way of a plan.

CHAPTER FOURTEEN

"I think we have to head downtown soon. The press conference will be starting in half an hour and we should get there before it begins," Connie said. She didn't mention the fact they were going to have to split up, if they had any hope of stopping Dirty Joe while she figured out what was going on with her parents.

Trusting her stepfather was pushing it, despite a very real and growing hope that she could. One thing was bankable; her mother wouldn't lie. If the e-mail had come from her, Connie could trust her mother wouldn't knowingly set her up.

"I just wish we had a solid plan to go on before we left," Barrett said before draining his coffee mug.

"Same here, but we still have the ride downtown to talk," she offered. Every minute was precious and could be used to their benefit. The thought extended out to more than just this situation. Life was precious, and she was beginning to see how much so. A little voice in the back of her mind said she should grab hold of every chance at happiness. There were no guarantees. Life had an expiration date for everyone, and she could see clearly now that she had been existing instead of living. The future, *her* future, would be so much brighter if Barrett was involved.

When it was all said and done, she needed to have a conversation with him to see if he was on the same page. Because if he was, she didn't want to walk away from whatever this was that was developing between them. The thought of living without him caused a physical ache. She paused. Could this be love?

She'd never allowed anyone into her heart before, but then there'd never been anyone as special as Barrett in her life.

He'd been clear about his commitment to a single life. Was it possible there've been changes in him too? If someone had told Connie she would meet and fall deeply in love with someone in the space of a couple of days, she would have told them they'd lost their minds. And yet, here she was doing just that. Or were her emotions heightened because she was in a life or death situation? Logic agreed with the latter. Her heart said it wasn't even a remote possibility. Could her emotions lead the way? Throw caution aside and just *feel* her way through?

It was a foreign feeling at best to trust her emotions and open her heart to someone. Time would tell if she was even capable. It was in short supply and running out. She could only hope both of them would make it through today alive.

"Are you hungry?" Barrett asked. "This might be the last chance to eat for a while."

"I couldn't eat a bite," she said, shaking her head. "The coffee will hold me over until we get through this." She thought about what Barrett had said about making plans for the future as though everything would work out in the next few hours. "In fact, I think we should all meet back here for a late dinner."

There was a moment of silence between the brothers, as though they needed time to process what she was really saying. And then both heads nodded.

"I'll make sure the others know," Harding stated as Barrett reached for her hand and then gave a gentle squeeze. The sweet reassurance sent a jolt of electricity up her arm and straight to her heart.

"It's a date then," she said before turning to face Barrett. "Ready?"

"As much as I'll ever be," he said, then came the small smile that upturned the corners of his lips.

"Then, let's do this so we can hurry and get back," she said.

Harding laid a twenty-dollar bill on the table as they pushed to standing. He placed a valet ticket in the palm of Barrett's hand for their new ride.

Strangely, she would miss the Chevy. There'd been something freeing about riding in a vehicle that had been made before Bluetooth technology and smart cars. The vintage vehicle reminded her of a simpler time—a time she wanted to hang onto as much as possible.

When had life become so complicated? She missed those carefree days in Crickett, with Mitchel bugging her to play ball. Her baby brother would drag her onto the court where he had obstacle courses set up for them to ride their bikes on. He set up ramps that she'd refused to try. Instead, she cheered him on from the sidelines as he attempted 'death defying' tricks; she would be the commentator while her brother assumed the daredevil role.

Missing Mitchel had always stopped her from thinking about him. Remembering had caused a pain so deep, so raw, that she felt like she would never recover. Her response was to bury the memories along with the pain. But it never really went away. She was realizing that all she had was the pain, without the joy of remembering all the good times. What a shame, she thought, because there had been so many beautiful times while Mitchel had been alive. He'd done more living in his short time on this earth than most did in a lifetime.

And he would be sad if he knew what she'd become. Too careful with her life. Too careful with her heart. Too careful to let anyone in who might hurt her.

A rogue tear escaped and rolled down her cheek as they exited the bar. She wiped it away as she entered the lobby, and a man in a suit came rushing toward them. His shiny bronzed nametag said he was an employee. The suit said he was in management.

Barrett and Harding closed ranks, taking a step in front of her, essentially blocking the Suit's view of her. She immediately knew why they'd done it. His gaze was locked onto her the whole time he was making a beeline toward them. She'd been recognized.

"Excuse me," Suit said. He was in his mid-forties, if she had to guess. His hair was dark, except where it was graying at the temples. He was short by Quinn standards, probably around five feet ten inches, if she had to guess. His face held stress wrinkles that were etched into his forehead and in the form of brackets around his mouth.

"Can we help you with something?" Barrett asked.

"I would like to speak to Connie Owens, please," he said and her stomach sank. Clearly the man knew who she was, whereas she had no idea who Suit was, which meant he knew her stepfather.

"I'm right here," she said, emerging from behind the Quinn brothers. She forced a smile despite the staccato rhythm her heart was pounding out against her ribs. "What can I help you with?"

"I have a message for you," Suit began, and then in a whirlwind an immaculately dressed woman came rushing through the double glass doors of the lobby. Her heels clicked against the marble flooring as she raced toward Connie.

"Mother!" Connie said, the relief overwhelming her momentarily.

Her mother's arms opened wide as she neared, and the sheer look of relief on the woman's face warmed Connie's heart.

"You're alive," Mother said as she brought Connie into an embrace. Tears streaked her face, threatening to ruin her mascara. It was something she would have been concerned about in the past. Not now. The only thing that seemed to matter to Mother was Connie's well-being.

"I'm here," Connie whispered, closing her eyes as she hugged her mother right back. "And I'm not going anywhere. Not if I have anything to say about it."

She couldn't be certain how long the two of them stood there and couldn't bring herself to notice.

"Your father has been worried sick," Mother said, pulling back enough to lock gazes.

Connie didn't have it in her heart to correct her mother by saying stepfather, as she'd begun to do as an adult.

"What's going on, Mother?" Connie asked. She glanced around in search of Barrett as her heart threatened to explode.

Barrett and Harding were gone. Connie lost her balance as she tried to step toward the door, and her mother caught her. She couldn't let herself believe this could be the last time she would ever see Barrett alive again.

This seemed like the right time to remind herself of their plan. They would meet back here for dinner. He would survive and his brother would live. Period.

———

Barrett borrowed a pen and slip of paper from the valet. He scribbled out a note to Connie and then gave the valet a crisp hundred-dollar bill to deliver the message to her once he was gone.

"Are you sure you don't want to drive together?" Harding asked as he waited.

"No. I got this," Barrett said, shaking his head. A dark cloud formed over his head and his heart at the thought of leaving the hotel without her. But this was better. He couldn't shoulder the risk of anything happening to Connie because she happened to be standing next to him. A stray bullet killed just as thoroughly as one that hit its intended target. He would never be able to live with himself if anything happened to her because of him. One look at Mrs. Owens had told him everything he needed to know about Connie's safety.

Connie was going to be fine. Her family would find a way through this. And he hoped that he could somehow fit into the picture once this whole ordeal was behind him, behind them.

Barrett had no idea if she felt the same, but he'd fallen in love fast and hard. Rather than tell her in the note, he made plans to tell her in person. He had no idea if the news would be welcome, but he had to know where he stood with her. He had to know if she would be willing to give their relationship a shot. First, he had to survive.

Right now, Crawford had to take center stage. The valet brought the white four-door sedan to him before he slipped into the driver's seat and headed downtown on what should be a fifteen-minute drive. Parking was a whole other story. After the short drive, he found a spot in an apartment complex two blocks over in front of a fire hydrant, figuring the ticket would be well worth it. Time was a luxury at this point.

There was already a thick crowd gathering. Barrett ran through throngs of people, ignoring the throbbing pain in his right shoulder as his blood got pumping. Something was niggling at the back of his mind that he couldn't quite pinpoint.

"Excuse me," he said time after time as he maneuvered through the crowd. If folks thought driving in Austin was congested, they should try walking—or in his case running—through shoulder-to-shoulder crowds.

Anyone who'd attended a music festival would attest to the fact trying to get somewhere was like salmon swimming upstream during spawning season. Crowded didn't begin to describe this mess.

A thought tried to break through, but he couldn't quite access it as he produced his badge to part the sea of people a little faster. It was a risky move because it could easily draw attention to him, but not getting there in time could have a devastating effect for Crawford.

"U.S. Marshal," he said to the cop at the barricade. "Where's the chief?"

The cop shifted the barrier so that Barrett could slide through, and then motioned toward the makeshift podium in the parking lot of the apartments. All the vehicles had been cleared. The very real fear the governor would turn this into something political, even if it risked Crawford's life, sat heavy in Barrett's gut.

The ache in his chest at leaving Connie behind, without having a chance to explain, threatened to swallow him whole. He'd never experienced anything of this magnitude when it came to dating and he knew —probably had known since the moment he met her —that she was going to be something special in his life.

Barrett shoved those thoughts aside as he made his way toward the chief, badge flat against his palm. A niggling voice stopped him short of reaching the podium area, and followed eyes to the window where Crawford was being held hostage. No news was most definitely not good news.

He spun around, trying to figure out what could

possibly be bugging him to the point that something in his subconscious screamed at him.

And then it dawned on him.

Dirty Joe didn't want to be caught. He wouldn't draw attention to his exact location. No. He'd be somewhere close by, just like Barrett had been in the jungle, watching from a distance. Law enforcement would be on every rooftop, that would provide a decent vantage point for a shooter to take down anyone on the podium. This was all happening so fast they wouldn't have time to secure every window, though.

Barrett glanced around at the crowd that lined the barricades, thinking people needed to go home. They had no idea what would happen, but this scene definitely could end up a blood bath. Dirty Joe wanted one person...Barrett. And he was presently standing in plain view. How many others would the perp be willing to sacrifice to kill Barrett?

He moved back into the crowd, hunkering down so he could make himself as small as possible. Now that Dirty Joe had had a chance to identify what Barrett was wearing, he would look for the flannel. Barrett needed a new shirt. Since his overnight bag was still in the Chevy, there was no option there. For a split second, his thoughts shifted to Connie. He knew she was fine and, better yet, safe, but that still didn't stop him from missing her.

A big guy wearing a burnt orange hoodie caught Barrett's eye. He immediately reached for his wallet. The UT sweatshirt would blend into this crowd easily, essentially making him disappear. He would be a very difficult target if he could score one of those.

He moved toward Sweatshirt as he pulled five, crisp, one hundred dollar bills from his wallet. He tucked his wallet into his back pocket and gripped the bills.

"I'll give you five hundred dollars for your hoodie," he said to Sweatshirt.

Since the guy looked at Barrett like he had two heads, he held up the cash. "No strings attached. It's important that I have the sweatshirt."

"Why not go to literally any store and buy one?" Sweatshirt asked, but he was already shrugging out of the one he was wearing.

It was a legitimate question.

"No time," he said before flashing his badge. "I'm law enforcement, so I promise I'm not trying to do anything illegal."

The guy nodded and handed over the sweatshirt with a shiver as a cold breeze blew on them.

"How about we trade?" Sweatshirt asked.

"No can do, and I don't have time to explain. It's a cash only offer," Barrett said. "But you can replace this one at almost any store around here."

"Cool," the guy said as he took and then pocketed the money.

Barrett thanked him as he turned toward the barricade. He couldn't allow the guy to wear the flannel in case Dirty Joe had gotten a visual on Barrett before. No way would Barrett put the young man's life at risk so blatantly.

As he surveyed the windows opposite the platform, he caught a glimpse of a shadow crossing a window that had a perfect view of the podium and the apartment. Barrett bit back a curse as he methodically moved toward it, mentally calculating how long it would take him to reach the window as a representative for Austin PD took the makeshift stand.

Everyone's attention shifted toward the voice booming from the speaker that sat on the makeshift stage. Barrett would be instantly noticed if he didn't follow the crowd's lead, so he focused his eyes toward the apartment building where Crawford was being held. And then it dawned on him; there were two possibilities as to why Crawford hadn't escaped. Barrett couldn't allow himself to consider a third because Crawford had to be alive.

The first possibility was that Dirty Joe had enlisted a helper. The second was that a bomb was strapped to Crawford. *This will blow up in the face of everyone you love.* Barrett bit back a curse. That was the 'thing' that had been niggling at the back of his mind. Dirty Joe's last words as he was about to be led away. He'd been hinting at how he planned to take Barrett down. *Blow up.* A bomb.

Barrett looked around, scanning the faces of inno-cent men, women, and children. Those would haunt him for the rest of his life if he lived beyond today. Out of the corner of his eye, he saw a pair of kids being reunited with the babysitter from the news. Had they been used and released by Dirty Joe? Were they nothing more than insurance? And now being let go?

This area needed to be cleared and a robot needed to be sent into the apartment. *Now!* Barrett pulled out his cell phone and called Harding. It took two minutes to explain his theory. Less than that for Harding to respond with a promise to take the bastard down and keep Crawford safe.

"I'll pull the senator aside and explain the situation to him," Harding stated as tension radiated through the line.

"He might not believe you," Barrett warned. "We have no jurisdiction here and he is clearly not the most reasonable man."

"Don't worry, bro," Harding said. "The way to the senator's heart just walked by me. We got this."

Without a further explanation, Harding ended the call. Barrett had to trust his brother knew what he was doing. And he had to trust his own instincts about where to find Dirty Joe.

CHAPTER FIFTEEN

Connie searched the faces of the crowd that was lining the barricades, praying she could find Barrett's. He had to be here somewhere; she couldn't allow herself to believe anything bad had happened to him. Her heart was in her throat as her mother led her to where Hunter Owens III stood, his back facing her.

As they made a beeline toward him, someone tapped him on the shoulder no doubt alerting him to her presence. Her stomach twisted in knots as he turned. His tense expression immediately shifted to relief. Connie exhaled the breath she didn't realize she'd been holding.

She stopped a few feet short of her stepfather before folding her arms across her chest. He glanced around, nervous. Was he afraid someone would hear them? Because despite her mother's reassurances that he was innocent, Connie needed more than her mother's word.

"I can explain everything," her stepfather started,

his gaze finally meeting hers. There was a sincerity and vulnerability in his eyes where she normally saw confidence that bordered on haughtiness. "Can you trust me?"

"No," she said as honestly as she could. "That ship sailed a long time ago."

Her stepfather's security team moved into action, encircling them.

"Then, do you mind stepping a little closer?" he asked. There was a quality to his voice she barely recognized in him...humility.

"That, I can do," she said, and then closed the distance between them until they were standing almost toe-to-toe. With her mother by her side, Connie's confidence she could trust the situation and her instincts grew considerably. The changes in her stepfather's expression—the kindness and remorse there—wasn't something he could get away with faking. Not with Connie. She knew him too well. Another emotion was present behind his eyes too. One she instantly recognized...fear.

"This is all my fault," he started in a refreshing change of pace.

"What is?" she asked.

"What happened to you," he said as moisture gathered in his eyes. He cleared his throat and looked to be holding back his emotions by sheer force of will. There were cameras around via the media and cell phones. The old Hunter Owens III would have used this moment to 'show' he cared. The new one seemed embarrassed and a little caught off guard at the intensity of his emotions. "I made a wrong move with a man named..." He glanced around before leaning toward her and covering his mouth. "Thorogood Hammond."

"The businessman?" she asked, but it was more statement than question. "I've seen him all over the news lately. Isn't he in some financial trouble?"

"Yes," he said. "Turns out, he'd brought on investors to build on public land over by Zilker Park. He used their money to pay off some of his other debts so his construction business could stay afloat."

"Sounds like robbing Peter to pay Paul," she said. "And a dangerous strategy."

"You hit the nail on the head there," he admitted, his expression hinting at pride. "The problem is that no legitimate financial institution would give him a loan, so he turned to other folks and then used them as leverage to pressure me to pass legislation to allow the project to move forward."

"They stood to make a fortune, considering there's no stone left unturned in Austin development," she said, realizing what a huge money-maker a project like that one could be.

"The money would come in hand-over-fist. Hammond figured he could cut into his own profit to pay off his loans and no one would be the wiser," he stated.

"Why not go along with it?" she asked, thinking it would have been easy enough. Sure, there would have been a public backlash. A skilled politician like her step-father would have been able to figure out a way to spin the legislation to make his constituents believe he was doing Austin a favor.

"I know I've done things in the past...things I

deeply regret," he began, "but I really did get into office to serve. I lost sight of what was important along the way. This showed me how far I'd gone. Hammond would only target a senator he believed could be bought off." He compressed his lips as he frowned. "That's what I'd become."

"Was he wrong?" she continued.

"This has been one of the most eye-opening experiences of my life," he stated with conviction. "I'm not that kind of person or representative, which is why he targeted you instead."

Her eyebrow shot up.

"Hammond decided the best way to get to me was to use you," her stepfather explained. "He sought to discredit you and use the pictures as blackmail to get me to do his bidding. He basically outlined his plans in a not-so-veiled threat."

"And you told him to go right ahead and do it," she said, realizing this is the part she'd overheard. "In fact, you told him that my death would only make you more popular."

"A stupid attempt to convince him that your life didn't matter to me in order to protect you," he admitted. "Hammond saw right through it, though."

She nodded. His explanation matched up with what she'd overheard.

"Can I see your phone?" she asked.

He nodded before handing it over.

Connie pulled up the news story about the motorcycle man. His face, bruised and swollen, sat below the headline. "Do you recognize him?"

Her father's eyes widened as he nodded. He seemed to quickly skim the article as she handed back his cell.

"Judd Wielding," her father said. "He's a known associate of Hammond's son."

She chewed on the information for a second, which was about all the time she had as nervous tension seemed to build in the crowd around them.

"How can I trust that you've changed?" she asked, figuring honesty was the first step toward repairing their relationship. She was still undecided as to whether or not that was even possible at this point. This was merely keeping the door open.

"There was another reason that I could never compromise that land." He flashed eyes at her. "A personal one."

Connie tightened her grip on her elbows.

"Zilker Park was the first place the three of us went after I adopted you," he said as the moisture welled in his eyes. "After Mitchel came along, it became one of his favorite places to go. The area has such a special meaning to our family that I could never vote to destroy the land even if I was a lousy father in every sense of the word otherwise. It was the one thing I hung onto even when I knew I'd lost you."

A tsunami of emotion threatened to drag Connie under, chew her up, and spit her out.

"You didn't have to lose me," she said, the heaviness she'd carried around in her chest over their strained relationship started breaking up.

"After losing Mitch, I became afraid of losing you too," he said. "Stupidly, it caused me to push you away and I can see that so clearly now. I lost you by being a jerk and there isn't a day that goes by that I don't think about you and your brother or regret my actions when I was in pain. It was just so all-consuming. I mistakenly believed being tough was for the family's own good. That I needed to be strong for you and your mother. Inside, I was a wreck and in hindsight acted like a jerk."

"I moved out," Connie's mother interjected in a shocking revelation. "We don't live together any longer."

Her gaze dipped down to her mother's wedding finger to find nothing but a tan line there.

"I'm not sure the marriage can be saved," her mother admitted with a shrug.

"Then, I'm confused about why you're here." Connie's gaze bounced from her mother to her stepfather. His face muscles tensed.

"I don't deserve forgiveness from either of you. Your mother has graciously agreed to give us another chance as long as we take it slow. I'd like the opportunity to be a better husband, father, and man. However, I'll understand and respect your decision if there's no going back for you, Connie."

Connie didn't have to think long and hard about her next move. Everyone ought to have a second chance if they were sincere in their apology and committed to change.

"Forgiveness won't be easy, but if you truly mean those words, count me in," she said, releasing what had felt like the weight of the world with those words.

"Thank you," he said with a graciousness and gratitude that had been missing far too long. "I hope it's okay to say how proud I am of you. And that I understand my actions and mine alone caused my marriage and family to be where it is today."

"Words can't erase the past," she reminded, "but the past doesn't have to predict the future."

"That's up to the three of us," her mother chimed in with the first genuine smile Connie had seen in a long time.

Only time would tell if fences could be mended within their small family. She glanced around and saw Harding making a beeline toward them. As the reality of Barrett's situation came crashing down on her, she realized time was running out.

After quick introductions, Harding started right in.

"We have reason to believe there's a bomb upstairs," he stated before turning toward Connie's stepfather. "We need your help."

"Why not go to the chief?" he asked.

"There's not a whole lot of time to convince him, sir," Harding stated matter of fact.

"Going over the head of the chief of police isn't exactly going to make me popular with the man," her stepfather pointed out.

"I can appreciate the position this puts you in," Harding said with compassion. "My brother is up there in that apartment that might blow sky-high any minute. There are a whole lot of innocent people who don't deserve to die today, including you and your family."

"Where is he?" Connie asked as panic gripped her. "Where's Barrett?"

"He said this is between him and Dirty Joe. All he said is that he thinks he found him," Harding said with a sharp sigh. Tension lines scored his forehead, and it was easy to see how much he loved his brothers.

"Dad..." Connie tried to regulate her breathing, but it was impossible at this point. "Please, help."

She didn't want to ruin his career if the intel was bad. However, not doing anything when they had a chance to save all these lives couldn't be an option.

"Sir?" Harding shifted his weight from one foot to the other as he caught her stepfather's gaze.

"How do you know there's a bomb threat?" her stepfather asked.

"I don't have proof," Harding admitted. "But this is more than a hunch. The perp threatened to blow up everyone who was important to my brother at the arrest."

"Why would he blow up the building he was in?" her stepfather asked. Connie had the same question.

"He wouldn't," Harding admitted. "There would be no satisfaction in dying along with the people close to my brother. We believe the perp is in a nearby building watching, but don't look up right now."

Connie's stepfather played it cool, looking down at the ground as he nodded as though he was being briefed on the situation instead of being asked to pull rank and put his reputation on the line.

"I realize this is a big ask," Harding continued. "And I can't guarantee that we're one hundred percent on target. What I can tell you is that if we are and the perp sees my brother...it's game over. All these lives are gone." He snapped his fingers. "Like that."

"While the police chief and several senators stood around and did nothing," her stepfather added.

"Yes, sir," Harding said. "Depending on the size of the bomb..."

He didn't finish the sentence. Didn't need to for her stepfather to get the point.

"What do you recommend that I do?" he asked Harding.

"Call the chief over and tell him to send in a robot. Quietly. No one can know about this until it's done. Anything else will jeopardize the lives of my brothers," he explained.

"Okay," her stepfather said. "Let's do this."

CHAPTER SIXTEEN

Barrett moved through the crowd, making his way toward the apartment building on the opposite side of the parking lot while trying not to draw attention to himself. This was not an easy feat considering he must look like salmon swimming upstream to an onlooker. To counter the effect, he moved around the perimeter of the crowd as much as possible.

A bomb could be detonated from any location, but Dirty Joe would want to sit back and watch. Cell phones had come into popularity with criminals since they were terrorist favorites to trigger improvised explosive devices, aka IEDs. The benefit of a cell was obvious. A bomb could be detonated from a remote location. The perp could be miles away and, therefore, impossible to tie to the event.

He exhaled a couple of breaths before taking in a slow one after reaching the building. His target was on the third floor, camped out next to the window. That was the assumption Barrett was making. There were a whole lot of unknowns that made this one-man operation even more dangerous. Forget about his own life, except when it came to Connie. She made him want to come home to someone every night...to her.

Then there was Crawford to consider as well as the crowd. Barrett was low on options. Going directly to his brother would be a mistake, which didn't mean his current path wasn't. Cell phone detonators could be dealt with, given enough time. The feds had to be involved to use cell phone jamming equipment. But even that couldn't stop a cell phone's alarm function from doing the job. So, yeah, short on options.

The building's front door was made of glass. Barrett expected the door to be locked but tried it anywhere. Some places only locked at night. *Bingo!* The door opened. Barrett slipped inside. He located the stairwell and the elevator before familiarizing himself with the ground floor layout. Apartments with north facing windows were to the right of the hallway.

Barrett was very aware of the fact he needed to catch Dirty Joe unaware, or he'd press a button and blow up Crawford along with many innocent civilians. Figuring out how to surprise the man was a hat trick in and of itself.

An idea popped as he crested the second floor. He exited the stairwell and calculated approximately where the apartment above would be located. The place was center to the building, so that meant 3C as there were only five apartments on either side of the hallway on each floor.

The floor below was apartment 2C. Barrett wrapped on the door with his knuckles. A youngish man, early thirties, answered on the first knock. Barrett immediately flashed his badge.

"Sir, I have reason to believe there is an imminent threat to this building," he stated as a woman holding an infant in her arms cautiously approached. "You and your family need to vacate the premises immediately. Go as far in the opposite direction of the action as you can get."

For a split second, the image of the little family morphed into him and Connie. She held their baby in her arms. Normally, an image like this would haunt Barrett. In this case, it provided comfort and warmth as though a hundred tiny campfires had been lit inside his chest.

"Honey," the woman said as the man stood there as though sizing up Barrett to make sure he wasn't off his rocker with a fake badge.

"Believe me when I tell you to go," Barrett reassured, using his authoritative law enforcement tone. Folks in shock—and that seemed to be the case here—responded to authority.

"All right," the man finally said before glancing back at his wife and child.

Barrett's cell buzzed in his pocket. He fished it out and placed the volume on complete silence mode. Then, he checked the message from Harding and his chest squeezed. The image from the robot's camera was that of Crawford bound to a chair with a bomb strapped to his chest.

"You guys need to hurry," was all he said as he stood at the door. He needed to get them out. Now.

Tiny beads of sweat formed on Barrett's forehead as the family raced past him. "I need to enter your apartment for official business. Can I have your permission to enter?"

"Yes," the wife said as her husband ushered her toward the elevator. "Please, be careful."

"Always," he said before closing the door behind him and cutting across the room to window.

He glanced outside. Thankfully, no one seemed to be paying attention to anything other than the apartment across the lot. With his cell phone still out, he fired off a text to Harding, who stood next to the senator and Connie. She was too close to the building. If it blew, both her and Harding would go up with it.

Grab Connie and get out of here.

He watched as his brother checked his cell phone. Harding shook his head before showing the message to Connie. Her response was the same as his brother's. They weren't going anywhere.

Make sure no one looks this way.

His second text received a couple of nods. Good. Because he was about to turn into Spiderman and no one could notice if he was going to pull this off. Dirty Joe would have the window cracked so he could hear the crowd, and revel in the devastation. He would want to milk this victory by essentially sticking up a middle finger to all law enforcement agencies. He'd killed another one of their own and put another feather in his proverbial cap. He was trying to make it known to the world that he was untouchable.

His ego might end up being his biggest downfall.

The senator stepped up to the microphone, drawing all eyes toward him. Barrett made his move, climbing out the opened window. He gripped the bricks and used the ledge as leverage for his feet. At his height, with his arm reach, the window above wasn't unreachable with a little effort. White hot pain ripped through his shoulder.

Barrett clenched his back teeth. *Grin and bear it, Quinn.*

Reaching for the sill caused him to release a grunt as he scaled the building. He'd been in tricky situations during his career. This ranked right up at the top, dwarfing all others.

His brother's life literally rested in his hands. The woman he loved along with Harding was in the crowd below—a crowd that would end up collateral damage if he made one wrong move.

The robot across the street would take time to diffuse the bomb on its end. With the situation heating up, a crescendo was nearing. Barrett could feel it in his bones.

Dirty Joe was a patient man. He was calculating in his business affairs, some might even call him meticulous. He'd been plotting, planning since his arrest. The dirtbag needed to go down and *stay* down this time. Barrett bit back a whole string of swear words, reminding himself he would only draw unwanted attention. As it was, onlookers focused on the apartment across the street where the senator was delivering an impassioned address.

Barrett moved methodically, just like when he

climbed. The lack of a belay to anchor him should he lose his grip wasn't something he decided to focus on.

As he'd noted earlier, the windowsill was cracked in apartment 3C. Barrett climbed to the side of it and listened over the booming voice of the senator.

The sound of a toilet flushing caught his attention. Seriously? Could the man's bladder be the reason he went down twice? The irony caused Barrett to smile through the pain on his shoulder. He gritted his teeth rather than make a noise as he jumped into action.

The cell was just inside the apartment, halfway across the small living room, sitting on the couch's armrest. Barrett forced the window open as the spigot in the bathroom turned on. He pushed through blinding shoulder pain as he twisted around for the climb inside.

The water stopped and a second later, the bathroom door opened. Barrett was halfway to the cell when Dirty Joe spotted him. Barrett drew his weapon as he dove toward the cell. As Dirty Joe reached behind his own back, Barrett stretched out his hand toward the phone.

Dirty Joe smirked as he came around with a weapon. Barrett's hand smacked against the carpet, opened, and the cell tumbled out. He had a second to make a choice. Go for the cell or find cover before Dirty Joe fired.

Barrett tucked and rolled, screaming out in pain as his shoulder made contact with the flooring. He managed to put sheetrock between him and a bullet. Popping to his feet, groaning the whole way, he couldn't allow Dirty Joe to reach the cell first.

Weapon in hand and leading the way, Barrett shouted, "Hands where I can see 'em."

An icy chill ran down his back at the calmness in Dirty Joe's voice when he said, "I don't think so."

Barrett had two options. Stay where he was and live while his brother and many of the people he loved were killed. Or risk his own hide to save everyone outside that window.

Before Dirty Joe could get to the phone, Barrett came around the corner and fired. Dirty Joe spun around as survival instinct must have kicked in, forcing him to retreat. Barrett tucked and rolled, coming up with the cell along the way. He tucked it underneath the bookshelf before pulling out his own and palming it. "Come out with your hands up, Joe," Barrett demanded. "We both know this apartment is about to be filled with so many law enforcement officers it'll feel like one of those ant farms where we'll be climbing over each other. There's no way out for you except in handcuffs."

"We both know those don't hold me for long," he countered.

"Then, I'll come after you again and again," Barrett stated, his voice laced with confidence he didn't feel. "Come out. Hands up. It's the only way."

"Not from my viewpoint," Dirty Joe stated before firing a shot.

His intentions clicked with Barrett instantly. The wild shot wasn't wild at all. It was calculated to keep Barrett away while Dirty Joe exited out of the bedroom window.

Following his instincts honed by years of experience and training, Barrett barreled down the hallway and to the bedroom door. Back against the wall, leading with his weapon, he risked a glance.

Dirty Joe had the window open and was straddling the sill. He made the mistake of looking down, which gave Barrett the couple of seconds he needed to cross the room, grab two fistfuls of shirt, and yank the bastard back inside.

The perp came tumbling down on top of Barrett, right on his bad shoulder. Blood soaked his shirt as Dirty Joe's gaze locked onto the weakness. He stabbed his fingers into the wound, and Barrett nearly came unglued. He grunted and let out a scream as his hand opened and his cell phone tumbled out of his grasp.

He expected a barrel to his forehead as he'd lost his weapon. When none came, he suspected Dirty Joe had let go of his in the fall.

Fighting against the pain that threatened to drag him under, Barrett alligator rolled until they hit a wall and he was on top. The look on Dirty Joe's face when he thought he was about to win would be etched in Barrett's mind forever. The upturned corners of his lips that said, "Gotcha!" were immediately replaced with a frown as he seemed to realize he wasn't holding his own phone.

"You didn't think I was that stupid, did you?" Barrett asked, capitalizing on the split second of shock that seemed to freeze his opponent.

With all of his strength, Barrett reared back and slugged Dirty Joe across the jaw. His head snapped to one side, his eyes fluttered, and blood came dripping out of his mouth. Barrett seized the opportunity to roll Dirty Joe face down on the carpet while scanning the immediate area for a weapon. There was only a shiny metal object within spitting distance. Barrett couldn't reach it without removing pressure on Dirty Joe, so he kicked it far out of reach.

Grabbing his cell phone after checking to ensure Dirty Joe was unconscious, he fired off a text to Harding with their exact location. Barrett wouldn't breathe easy until Dirty Joe was in cuffs again.

It only took a matter of minutes for the thunder of half a dozen officers to fill the hallway, and then the apartment. Two officers relieved Barrett, handcuffing Dirty Joe while simultaneously searching the man for more weapons.

"His cell phone is underneath the bookshelf in the living room," Barrett stated as he tried to catch his breath. He'd propped himself against the bedframe with the help of one of the officers.

"EMT is on his way," the officer said to Barrett, who nodded. He'd expended all his energy in the fight and needed a minute.

Dirty Joe was yanked to his feet as his eyes blinked open. He searched the faces before finally settling on Barrett's.

"You think you won, but you didn't," was all Dirty Joe said before headbutting the officer to his left while simultaneously kicking the officer to his right. Before either officer could regroup, Dirty Joe bolted toward the opened window and then jumped headfirst.

"Sonofa—" Barrett stopped himself right there. He managed to push up to standing and stumbled toward the window. He braced himself at the sill. Then smiled.

A tree had broken Dirty Joe's fall. He wasn't dead. But the bones in his legs stuck out at odd angles, possibly shattered. The man wasn't going to be doing any more running for the rest of his life. No, he would be locked up and justice would finally be served.

Barrett searched the crowd for his brothers and Connie through blurry eyes. Found none of them. He turned and slumped against the wall.

CHAPTER SEVENTEEN

The crowd turned toward the man who'd jumped out of a third-story window. Connie had watched in horror as he'd landed on the top of a tree, then rolled down until he was in shrubbery before smacking against the sidewalk.

Pandemonium struck around Connie the second shock wore off the crowd. Parents covered their children's eyes as screams bounced off the buildings. The crowd surged, and Connie couldn't get a look at who'd come out the window. It had all happened so fast and came out of the blue that her brain couldn't process.

The next thing she knew, Harding had thrown his arm around her and, hunkered down, moved them both purposefully through the throngs of people. Her heart pounded the inside of her ribcage so hard she thought her chest might crack open. Barrett had to be alive. He had to be safe.

Harding strong-armed their way toward the building and headed straight for the glass door while saying something she couldn't quite make out over the noise around her. She could only pray Barrett wasn't the person who'd practically shot out the window minutes ago. At this point, all she knew for certain was the bomb had been diffused and Crawford was going to be fine. He was with the chief for a debriefing before the leader of Austin PD planned to deliver a statement to the media.

Crawford was alive because of Barrett's quick thinking and Harding's actions. The two made a great team and their bond reminded her so much of the thick-as-thieves relationship she'd had with Mitchel. Thinking about her brother didn't make her sad this time. In fact, remembering him and the closeness they'd shared flooded her with warmth.

Once the glass doors closed behind her, the outside noise faded.

"He's alive but hurt," Harding said with an apologetic look as they raced toward a stairwell.

The door opened behind them and a pair of EMTs holding a gurney rushed inside.

"Excuse us," they said in unison as Harding backed up against the wall to allow passage. Connie immediately followed his lead.

The stone-faced pair made a beeline for the stairwell. The tension on their faces caused all of Connie's muscles to tense up.

"Everything okay up there?" Harding asked as the men came flying past.

"We got an officer down," the second EMT stated before they disappeared.

"Doesn't mean it's him," Harding said out of the side

of his mouth. His tone came across as more hopeful than confident.

Connie reminded herself to breathe as a tsunami of emotions threatened. "Where is he?"

"Third floor based on the last time I heard from him," Harding said as they started toward the stairs again.

"How long ago was that?" she asked before those last words struck.

He shook his head as they hit the base of the stairs. Even with carpeting, she could hear feet shuffling above them. The sounds no doubt coming from the EMTs who were ahead of them. No one else had gone into the stairs to her knowledge and it only made sense they would still be climbing toward the third floor.

Connie couldn't allow herself to think Barrett was gone. But why wasn't he in contact with his brother?

"Doesn't mean anything," Harding said as though he could read her thoughts. It dawned on her that he was most likely going down that same path mentally—the one where Barrett was up there bleeding out. He'd already been injured in the shoulder. There'd been shots fired from this floor minutes ago. EMTs were racing upstairs.

None of which painted the best possible picture for Barrett being safe and alive.

"He might be giving his statement and, therefore, unable to answer," Harding said as they reached the second floor. Again, the hope in his voice shattered any possibility that he truly believed what he was saying.

They both knew Barrett would connect with his

brother if he was able to. A tiny piece of Connie's ego wanted to believe he would check on her the minute Dirty Joe was neutralized. It had to have been him flying out the window now that she knew it couldn't have been Barrett.

A little voice in the back of her mind picked that moment to say that Barrett would if he could. Was it wrong? Was she wrong?

She was about to find out as they crested the third story.

———

To say the wind had been knocked out of Barrett was a lot like saying a tornado was nothing more than a hard breeze. Thankfully, he was still conscious as an officer held a towel against Barrett's shoulder to stem some of the bleeding until the EMTs arrived.

Was he lightheaded? He could admit to seeing a few stars.

"Has anyone seen my cell phone?" he asked Officer Macintosh. Dark hair and eyes, serious expression, the officer had introduced himself as one of the men on the scene who'd let the perp slip right out of his hands. He'd been the one to take the unexpected kick. Barrett had reassured Officer Macintosh that Dirty Joe was one slippery son of a gun. He'd also informed the young officer that two U.S. Marshals had been killed while transporting the perp. So, he was doing better than he thought by still being alive.

No officer took the passing of fellow law enforcement easily. There was a brotherhood among them that tied them together as family, which made it all that much more difficult when one went rogue. Macintosh was one of the good guys and he'd taken the news to heart. He'd twisted a gold band around his ring finger without even realizing it was the first thing he'd done. Clearly, the man had immediately thought about his wife and the awful truth their jobs sometimes meant they wouldn't be coming home.

Then, he'd started working on Barrett by trying to stop the bleeding. Macintosh had requested a glass of water and a blanket, anything to make Barrett more comfortable when all he wanted to do was get up so he could go find Connie and his brothers.

A pair of EMTs came running in and toward him, blocking his view of everyone else in the room.

"Can you tell me your name?" one of the EMTs asked as he dropped down in front of Barrett.

"Barrett Quinn," he stated, figuring the guy had to ask his questions. "I'll be fine, by the way." He glanced over at his shoulder and noted the hand towel was soaked in blood. "It's just a scratch."

"I'm sure it is, sir," the EMT said. "My name is Mike and my partner here is Frankie. We plan to take good care of you."

Mike turned and whispered a few words to his partner.

"I'm trying to get information about my brothers," Barrett said. "And there's a woman with one of them."

"Is this guy giving you a hard time?" Harding's voice cut through the buzz and warmed Barrett's heart.

He craned his neck around to get a good look at Harding to see if Connie was still with him. Harding stepped aside as though he could read Barrett's mind. Then again, it was probably obvious.

His heart thundered in his chest at the thought of seeing her again.

"I'm here," came the voice he loved as Connie's beautiful face stepped into view. He broke into a wide smile as he waved her over. Staying awake was taking a whole lot more strength than he wanted it to. Seeing her again gave him the boost he needed to keep his eyes open when his lids felt like hundred-pound weights had been attached.

As Connie started toward him, the second EMT blocked her passage with an extended arm. The man was trying to do his job so there was no way Barrett would blast him. Before he could open his mouth to protest, Harding jumped into action. He was no doubt smoothing it over and doing a good job because the EMT gave a tight-lipped nod.

Connie rushed to him and dropped down to her knees. He reached for her hand, wincing in pain with movement. Okay, bad idea.

"Sorry," she said as she scooted closer so they could hold hands without him making much effort.

"No need to apologize," he said, "you're here." His gaze immediately flew to Harding. "Crawford?"

"Is safe. The intel you provided turned out to be spot-on, and the robot was able to diffuse the bomb and take it off Crawford before ka-boom town happened," Harding explained with a crack of a smile before turning serious. "You did it, bro. You saved our little brother and so many countless lives. I heard the mayor talking about giving you a medal on the way up here."

Harding winked, and Barrett realized his brother was jerking his chain.

He laughed and that hurt like hell.

"They probably will, though," Harding said with more sincerity this time. "You're a hero."

"The only prize I need is my brother alive, you here, and this beauty next to me," he quipped, realizing he'd spoken his heart in front of all these people. There was no question Connie had feelings for him. That didn't mean she wanted a relationship.

"Can you give my brother a little breathing room?" Harding said to the EMTs. His brother was practically a mind reader at this point. Actually, the two of them were just that close and had had each other's backs for so long the mind-reading bit wasn't exactly farfetched.

The EMTs grumbled but Harding reminded them that they were in the presence of a hero. The other officers in the room clapped, and they conceded defeat. The pair took a step toward the door, turning their backs on Barrett and Connie.

Connie's eyebrows drew together and a concern line scored her forehead.

"It's okay," he said to her, figuring he might as well go all-in at this point or risk losing her. "In fact, I've never been better. And there's one reason for that...*you*."

She smiled but her face was unreadable as to whether or not the feeling was reciprocated. She'd make one helluva poker player.

Barrett took in a deep breath, coughed, winced, and realized that had been a bad move. Since he was going for it, he continued, "If someone had told me that I could fall deeply, ridiculously in love with a person I'd barely met less than a week ago, I would have laughed. And, yet, that's exactly what just happened. You came into my life like a tornado, ripping down all the walls I'd built around my heart. Now? I can't imagine living a day without you. I've fallen for you. I love you. And I'd like to know if, someday, you'd consider doing me the incredible honor of marrying me?"

Putting his feelings out there should scare the heck out of him. Instead, it felt like the most natural thing in the world with Connie.

She squeezed his hand.

"For reasons I can't explain, I had a feeling you were going to be very special in my life when I first woke up in that hotel room," Connie began. "Did I know just what that meant at the time? Absolutely not." She paused and his heart skipped a couple of beats. "You see, in that moment, I didn't quite realize that I'd been waiting my whole life for you. My heart must have known the minute I woke up in that hotel room and laid eyes on you." She touched the center of her chest with his hand right at the place where he could feel her heartbeat. "This thing right here told me that you were something special then and I can't imagine a life without you now. To me, marriage is nothing more than a piece of paper, but if it's important to you, I'll marry you. I'm in this for forever, court documents or not."

If Barrett's heart could sing, it would belt out a love

song. Something Garth Brooks probably. Since it couldn't, he had to say the words out loud.

"I'll take whatever you'll give me, and we'll start with forever," he said to a round of applause from the room.

When his eyes closed this time, it was to kiss his future bride.

CHAPTER EIGHTEEN
Epilogue

Mother Nature seemed to be throwing out Powerball numbers these days instead of actual weather forecasts. The upcoming three-day string of warmth and sunny skies before a bitter storm hit were a high note. Since Crawford Quinn had been placed on paid leave following the bomb incident—an incident where he'd been caught off guard by a felon who was after his brother Barrett—it seemed like a good time to head home to Quinnland Ranch for some camping and fishing. Besides, he needed to find the re-set button. He was still fuming over a perp getting the drop on him. Granted, he'd do it all over again if faced with the same situation. Trading himself for innocent kids who'd been kidnapped had been a no-brainer. He was still scratching his head as to how the perp had known the trick would work. Was he that transparent?

If so, he'd better figure out a whole new line of work.

After three days, he had no idea what he was going

to do with his time. Finally paint the walls of the town-house he'd bought on a whim two years ago? Putting down roots was supposed to make Austin feel like home. And yet, nothing could compare to Quinnland.

The camping trip should help him get the ranch out of his system once and for all. It should give him a chance to catch his breath. And it should give him the space he needed to figure out his next move. Life seemed to be working against him on pretty much all fronts lately. Lady Luck seemed to be on the side of Mother Nature. Both had bad tempers directed mostly at him.

Fishing. He repeated the word a couple of times. What could possibly go wrong with that plan?

Click here to find out what happens to Crawford next.

ALSO BY BARB HAN

Don't Mess With Texas Cowboys

Texas Cowboy's Protection

Texas Cowboy Justice

Texas Cowboy's Honor

Texas Cowboy Daddy

Texas Cowboy's Baby

Texas Cowboy's Bride

Texas Cowboy's Family

Texas Cowboy Sheriff

Texas Cowboy Marshal

Texas Cowboy Lawman

Texas Cowboy Officer

Cowboys of Cattle Cove

Cowboy Reckoning

Cowboy Cover-up

Cowboy Retribution

Cowboy Judgment

Cowboy Conspiracy

Cowboy Rescue

Cowboy Target

Crisis: Cattle Barge

For more of Barb's books, visit www.BarbHan.com.

ABOUT THE AUTHOR

Barb Han is a USA TODAY and Publisher's Weekly Bestselling Author. Reviewers have called her books "heartfelt" and "exciting."

Barb lives in Texas--her true north--with her adventurous family, a poodle mix and a spunky rescue who is often referred to as a hot mess. She is the proud owner of too many books (if there is such a thing). When not writing, she can be found exploring Manhattan, on a mountain either hiking or skiing depending on the season, or swimming in her own backyard.

www.ingramcontent.com/pod-product-compliance
Lightning Source LLC
Chambersburg PA
CBHW071909220626
47052CB00002B/281